FEROCIOUS

JEFF STRAND

ISBN-13: 9781090993144

DISCLAIMER

The plausibility of this novel has not been verified by anybody in the scientific community, due to concern that their heads would explode.

CHAPTER ONE

Rusty didn't reach for his shotgun at the sound of the approaching car, but he did glance over at it. Though trespassers were rare and very unwelcome, he tried to give them the benefit of the doubt instead of immediately pointing a firearm at them and sternly suggesting that they get off his land. Oh, he'd point the shotgun at them early in the conversation; he simply made an effort not to start there.

He continued to sand the chair leg as he watched. The path to his cabin was long and winding and it would be another minute before the car arrived. If the driver was lost, he was *extremely* lost. It was virtually impossible to get lost enough to end up at Rusty's home. Visitors tended to be people who purposely ignored the posted signs, like that car full of obnoxious teenagers last year. That had been a very brief visit. He wasn't the type of person to be amused by cowardice, but watching those kids peel out and speed away had brought a small smile to his face.

The car, a fancy blue one, stopped in front of the

cabin. A thin guy in a nice shirt and tie got out of the vehicle. Rusty stood up, both to be polite and to be intimidating. He was not a small man.

"Rustin Moss?" asked the stranger.

"Rusty."

"You're a hard man to find."

"That's by design."

"I can see that. That road was...unfriendly. Not the right car for the job." The stranger walked up onto the porch and extended his hand. "I'm Grant Olander. I'm an attorney."

"You look like one."

Grant gestured to the chairs that filled half of the porch. "Did you make all of those?"

Rusty nodded.

"Nice work."

"Thank you."

"May I sit in one? Test it out?"

Rusty shrugged. "If you'd like."

Grant sat down in a rocking chair and rocked it back and forth a few times. "Oh, yeah. Now this is craftsmanship. None of that mass-produced garbage." He ran his fingers along the arm. "You can tell this was made by somebody who cared to do it right."

Rusty didn't like people very much, but admiring his furniture was one way to get on his good side. Not that he was going to offer the man a drink or anything. "I have to do quality work. It's how I make my living."

"You make a full-time living selling your chairs?"

"Not just chairs. I make tables, desks, dressers...but yes."

"Impressive."

Rusty shrugged. "I live cheap."

"Even so, it's great to be able to do what you love."

"Do you love being a lawyer?"

"I love being able to tell my parents I'm a lawyer."

"That's something."

Grant rocked a few more times, then frowned. "As you've probably guessed, I didn't drive all the way out here to test out a rocking chair. I'm here to deliver some bad news."

"I'm listening."

"Lori Richards is your sister, correct?"

"Yes."

"Which would make Flynn Richards your brother-in-law."

"That's right."

"They were in a car accident. Not their fault. The other driver ran a red light."

"Drunk?"

Grant shook his head. "Changing the radio station. Anyway..."

"Hold on," said Rusty. "I feel like I should sit down for the rest of this." He took a long, deep breath, then sat down on his fine homemade rocking chair.

"Your sister died instantly. She didn't suffer. The other car struck the passenger side head-on, and quite honestly she may not have even seen it coming. There are worse ways to go."

"Yeah." Rusty gritted his teeth as he clenched the armrests. A tear ran down his cheek, but he didn't care if the lawyer saw him cry. This was only the third time he'd cried in his adult life. Once per relative. "She wasn't even thirty yet."

"I know."

"What about her husband?"

"He didn't make it to the hospital."

Rusty had never even met his brother-in-law. Lori hadn't tried to make him feel guilty about not going to the wedding; it was on the other side of the country, and Rusty didn't do airplanes. She understood that. He wiped the tear from his eye. "What...what about...?"

"The baby?"

"Was it in the car?"

"Yes."

Rusty closed his eyes. "Goddamn it."

"The baby is fine. She was in a car seat in the back. A couple of scratches, and a piece of glass got her in the face but she was very, very lucky."

Rusty opened his eyes again. He wanted to smile and cry at the same time and he wasn't sure how to reconcile this. Conflicting emotions were not part of his world. He liked things to be simple.

Grant nodded toward his car. "Rusty, would you like to meet your niece?"

"I beg your pardon?"

"Your parents are deceased. You have no other siblings. You are Mia's only living relative."

"The baby's in the car?" asked Rusty, feeling a twitch of panic in his stomach. Babies were foreign and frightening.

"Yes."

"Right now?"

"Yes."

"Your car? The one that's right there?"

"I'll be back in a second." Grant gave the chair a couple more rocks, then got up and walked over to his vehicle. Rusty watched, his sorrow completely replaced by confusion and nervous tension. The baby was here?

Did that mean he was responsible for it? He did remember telling Lori that, yes, of course he'd be Mia's godparent, but he never thought his little sister would die!

Grant opened the back door and leaned into the car. He stayed like that for a few moments, which Rusty initially thought was a cruel effort to draw out the suspense, but then he realized that Grant was probably just undoing all of the straps on the baby seat.

Finally, Grant emerged with a baby in his arms. Beaming, the lawyer brought the pink-blanket-swathed child onto the front porch.

"Rusty, Mia. Mia, Rusty."

Rusty just gaped. He'd seen pictures, but all babies looked the same to him, so he couldn't be one hundred percent positive that this was his niece. She had a small bandage on her right cheek.

"Do you want to hold her?" Grant asked.

"Not at the moment, no."

Grant cooed at the baby, which was not something Rusty could ever do. He did not coo.

"This is obviously a great shock for you," said Grant, sitting down on the rocking chair. He began to rock gently, smiling at the baby as he did so. "If you weren't so far off the grid, of course we would have tried to give you some notice."

"Are you...are you *giving* her to me?"

"You're her godfather. Makes you sound like a crime boss, doesn't it? I completely understand that this is a lot for you to process all at once."

"Yes," said Rusty. "It really is."

"For what it's worth, she travels well. Barely cried at all on the trip over here."

"I can't be her dad. I don't know how to take care of a baby. I don't know how they work!"

"Oh, it's not that difficult. Just put food in one end and clean up the other end."

"I…"

"I apologize," said Grant. "I shouldn't be making jokes like that. You've just found out you lost your sister and now I'm here with this little bombshell. I'm not trying to make light of the situation."

"I can't do it."

Grant nodded. "You're not legally required to raise this child. It's not your baby."

"What would happen to her?"

"Foster care. She's a healthy child; she'll get adopted. You wouldn't be banishing her to an orphanage run by Mr. Bumble."

"Mr. Bumble?"

"From *Oliver Twist*. He ran the orphanage. He was very unpleasant."

"I remember him now."

"That would not be Mia's fate. She'll be fine, I promise you."

"Okay." This did not give Rusty any sense of relief, because he knew that he could not send this child away. He didn't believe in the afterlife, and so he didn't think that Lori was gazing down upon him at this moment. But he did believe in doing the right thing, and though he hadn't taken a blood oath and shouted *"I swear that I shall care for this child as my own!"* at the sky, he knew that it would devastate Lori to know that he'd simply abandoned her daughter to whatever the system chose to do with her. She might end up in a perfectly nice home with a perfectly nice family and live a perfectly nice life.

She might not.

Rusty and Lori rarely saw each other anymore. It was difficult to remain close with your sister when you'd pretty much eschewed all contact with other human beings except for a once-a-month trip to town to buy supplies and drop off furniture. Still, for eighteen years they'd been inseparable, and no way in hell was he going to go back on his word to her.

"I'll hold her now," he told Grant.

The lawyer stood up and carefully handed the baby to him. "Put your hand on the back of her head...yes, just like that...see, you've got it already."

Rusty looked down at Mia. She wasn't quite asleep but she was getting there. For an instant he thought that this might not be so bad, but then the aroma struck him.

"I think she has a dirty diaper," he told Grant.

"Yep. Gotta go." Grant hurried off the porch. Then he turned around with a grin. "I'm just kidding. I've got diapers and other supplies in the car. The first diaper change is on me."

"Thank you."

"I'm not going to chuck a kid at you and leave. If you come back with me, there are people who can help get you set up with what you need, answer the millions of questions I'm sure you have, and show you how to do things like change a poopy diaper. If you aren't able to do it now, I'll take Mia back to child services and she'll be cared for until you're able to join me and formalize everything."

"I never said I was taking her."

"I saw it in your face."

This answer surprised Rusty, because he assumed his face was a twisted mask of pure terror. Mia's eyes were closed now. Maybe all babies didn't look the same. Even with the bandage, she was way less ugly than most of the babies he'd seen.

He'd have to learn to coo.

"Do we need to schedule a different day?" Grant asked.

"Nah. I was just making a chair. It can wait."

"Excellent. It's going to be fine, Rusty. I'm not an optimist, believe me, but you've got this."

Grant went to his car and came back with an enormous box of diapers, which he joked was a half-day supply. He then apologized for the joke. He took Mia back from Rusty and asked to be directed to a good spot to change a diaper.

"Do you mind if I take a quick walk?" asked Rusty. "I don't think Lori's death has quite hit me yet, and I need some time to think. I promise it'll be quick."

"Take a long walk if you want. I'm enjoying the peace and quiet. Maybe I'll get you to hire me as a nanny."

"A quick one will do it. Thank you."

Rusty left his cabin and walked through the woods. He loved it out here. He really hoped that Mia did, too, because there was no way he was going to move back to the city. He'd have to make more frequent trips to town, he supposed, but that wasn't a major sacrifice. He'd handle her schooling himself, which meant that he had four or five years to learn history and geography and all of the other stuff he'd forgotten.

He wept for a while. He hadn't cried this hard when his mother and father died—also unfairly young—but he supposed it made sense that he'd be extra emotional at the moment.

Grant was right. It was going to be fine. Rusty had

this.

And if nothing else, Mia was going to have an *amazing* handmade wooden crib.

CHAPTER TWO

"**D**id you get tampons?" Mia asked. "You know I'll be menstruating soon."

Rusty maintained a stoic expression. She knew he hadn't forgotten the tampons. Their ongoing game was that she would frequently talk about feminine issues, knowing it made him extremely uncomfortable, and he would pretend that it did not bother him in the least. He always lost the game.

"I got them," he said. "I wouldn't want you to..." He started to make a disgusting comment, but couldn't force himself to say it out loud. Mia won again. "Thanks for sweeping up the place while I was gone."

Mia glanced at the wooden floor. "I *did* sweep it up."

"I know. That's why I thanked you."

"Oh. I thought you were being sarcastic."

"No, you're the sarcastic one in this family. Would you mind putting all the stuff away?"

"Sure. What are you going to do?"

"Watch you put all the stuff away."

Mia grinned and began to pull groceries out of the

13

bags. Rusty plopped down in his recliner, let out an exaggerated yawn, and stretched as if relaxing after a hard day of work, even though trips into town were not exactly brutal manual labor.

She'd been a tomboy for most of her youth, then in her teenage years entered a phase where she went in the opposite direction—all frilly dresses and makeup and long pretty nails. Now, at seventeen, she'd bridged the gap between the two. She wore blue polish on her short fingernails, spent too long every day fixing her hair, and wore a bit of makeup even though there was rarely anybody around but her Uncle Rusty.

Rusty was approaching fifty. His lifestyle kept him from getting soft, but the rapid metabolism that had served him so well for all of these years had finally abandoned him, so he'd acquired a gut that Mia did *not* make fun of because she knew he was genuinely sensitive about it. There was more gray in his hair than black now, but it looked all right, and he thought the creases gave a nice rugged look to a face that had never been particularly handsome. Overall, he could be doing a lot worse.

"Oooh, thanks!" said Mia, taking a package of red licorice out of one of the bags.

"I didn't say that was for you."

"You hate licorice."

"Maybe I've evolved. People change. They acquire experience and wisdom."

"Are you saying you've acquired new wisdom?"

"Oh, God no. I'm done with that shit."

Mia tore open the package and popped a stick of that nasty sugary crap into her mouth. She happily chewed on it while she put more stuff away.

"How's the bench going?" Rusty asked.

"Almost done."

"Really?"

"Really."

She could make furniture a lot faster than him now. It wasn't a "vibrancy of youth versus decrepitude of old age" kind of thing; she was faster than he'd been in his prime. One of the early lessons—one that took a while to make stick—had been to slow down and work with more care. Now she worked quickly *and* almost flawlessly.

Mia was also good at commissions. Rusty's process had always been to make whatever he wanted to make and then sell it. It had worked out well. He'd reluctantly take requests, but for the most part he preferred to simply drop off a load of furniture once a month and keep the human interaction to a minimum. Mia would talk to customers, get detailed descriptions of exactly what they wanted, and make it to their specifications. Sometimes they didn't quite know what they wanted ("Something that reminds me of Grandma") and Mia was able to figure that out, too. It was rare that anybody was less than thrilled with her work.

She was an excellent addition to the business. Which was good, because there wasn't a lot else for her to do out here. Having a baby dropped into his lap had required a significant lifestyle change, but he hadn't abandoned the core of what made him happy. He still lived in a cabin way the hell out in the middle of the woods. No Internet. No television. Almost no visitors.

They did have electricity. Pre-Mia, he'd fired up a generator in those rare instances when he needed it. Post-Mia, he'd gone to solar power, which had been expensive to install but had more than paid for itself after all these years. He'd added a whole new section to the cabin to give Mia her own room and some privacy. Though they still had the outhouse, which was Rusty's preferred venue for elimination, they also had an indoor flushable toilet. The whole place was more like a house than he would've wanted, but the disruption of his life had been almost all for the better.

Mia liked it out here. She didn't seem to mind that she was missing out on so much of the life of a normal teenaged girl. Sometimes, like today, she didn't even feel like going into town. Sure, they got on each other's nerves on occasion, but there was a *lot* of available wilderness for them to get some alone time. As far as Rusty was concerned, she could live with him for the rest of his life, and then have the cabin for the rest of hers.

That said, there were times when he felt guilty. Felt that he was robbing her of experiences that could define the direction of her life. She was damn good at making things, but what if she could cure diseases? What if she could invent things that changed lives? Or, hell, forget about her potential; was it fair that she'd never watched a movie?

This was something he needed to speak with her about. He'd tried to start the conversation several times and couldn't bring himself to do it. On the drive back from town, he'd vowed to do it today. And he would. As soon as she finished putting everything away.

When she finished putting everything away, he decided that their talk could wait for another hour or so. Maybe a day. Not more than a couple of days, though.

"What's wrong?" asked Mia, sitting down across from him at the table and popping her seventh piece of licorice into her mouth.

"Nothing's wrong."

"Ask me if I believe you."

"Do you believe me?"

"No. What's wrong?"

"Let's go for a walk."

"Oh, shit. This sounds serious." Mia had always been allowed to curse around him, though after one very embarrassing experience in the grocery store when she was seven, he'd had to explain that there were certain words only to be used at home.

"It's not," Rusty told her. "I mean, it *is*, but it's not bad."

"Let's go then."

They left the cabin. It was a beautiful September day, the kind when even the most hardcore city slicker would be envious of their living situation. There were eight different paths around the cabin, not counting the actual road, and Rusty decided that this conversation called for the long, straight path down to the creek. He took his niece's hand as they walked.

"What's up?" she asked.

"It's something I've been thinking about a lot lately. You're almost eighteen. The Amish have this thing—I can't remember the name, but there's a name for it—where kids your age go out into the real world for a couple of weeks. They see what else is out there. At the end of that time, they decide if they want to go back to being Amish, or if they want to leave that behind and stay in the real world."

"Okay," said Mia. It was a rare instance of Rusty not being sure what she was thinking.

"I don't want you to leave," Rusty told her. "My hope is that you'd come back from this and say that you agree with me that the real world is a bunch of crap. But I don't think it's fair to keep you away from everything without giving you a chance to see it for yourself and decide."

"I've seen the real world," said Mia.

Rusty shook his head. "No, you've seen this tiny little town. The world has a lot to offer. I hate it all, but that doesn't mean you will."

"Are you making me go?"

"No. I'm strongly suggesting that you go."

"Will you come with me?"

"No."

"I'm not going to just wander a big city by myself."

"That's not how it would work," said Rusty. "We wouldn't throw you to the wolves. You'd have a guide."

"It sounds awful," she informed him. "It seems like a good way for me to get stabbed to death."

"You won't get stabbed."

"Or hooked on drugs. Or pregnant. I can see myself not being able to resist peer pressure."

"We wouldn't be sending you out there to make bad choices. You'd still use common sense. I was thinking more that you'd go to see some live theater, eat at a fancy restaurant, go to a museum—that kind of thing. Go to a spa. Maybe, I don't know, go to a club and meet some people who aren't me. Make sure that the life I've chosen for us is the life you want to live."

"A spa sounds nice," said Mia.

"It sounds like hell on earth to me. People rubbing on you, putting green gook on your face. But you should try it. I don't want you to be seventy years old and spitting on my tombstone every day because I stole your life from you."

"You'd better still be alive when I'm seventy."

"Eighty, then."

"Eighty works."

"Again, I swear I'm not trying to get rid of you. I'll be—" Rusty almost said *heartbroken* but decided to tone it down a bit. "—sad if you leave. But you're almost an adult, and you need to be able to make an informed decision."

They walked silently for a moment. Mia let go of his hand, wiped some perspiration off on her jeans, then took it again.

"All right. I'll go. But I'll be back."

"I hope you will be."

"When are we going to do this?"

Rusty shrugged. "We don't have to set an exact date yet. We'll start making plans."

"Okay. Maybe it'll be fun."

"It will be. Just not as much fun as hanging out with your Uncle Rusty."

When she was very young, he'd toyed with the idea of having her call him "Dad," but decided against it. It seemed disrespectful to her deceased father. "Uncle Rusty" was fine.

They walked without talking for a few minutes until they heard the water. It was a fairly large creek, not as good for fishing as the pond, but it was a shorter walk and Rusty loved the sound. Two poles and a tackle box were always out here; nobody was going to steal them.

Mia let go of his hand again. "What's that?"

She hurried up ahead. Rusty picked up his pace, but at fifty he was perfectly content to let Mia be the first to make the discovery.

It was a dead deer, lying half in and half out of the

creek.

That is, the bottom half of the deer was in the creek, while the top half was scattered around about a fifteen-foot area.

Finding dead animals out here was rare. Nature cleaned itself up pretty quickly. That said, finding a dead deer would have elicited no more than an "Oh, that's interesting," except for the sheer carnage on display. This wasn't how animals died in the wild. Wolves would tear a poor creature apart, but this...this was like a thrill kill.

"What do you think happened?" asked Mia, walking right up to the scene of the crime. Despite his love of the primitive life, Rusty preferred to buy most of his meat from the grocery store. Still, they did some hunting, and Mia had dressed more deer carcasses than the average seventeen-year-old girl, so seeing this was unusual but not stomach churning.

"No idea." Rusty didn't even see the deer's head at first, then noticed it lying upside-down next to a tree.

"Maybe a bear got it?"

"A bear wouldn't fling the pieces around like this."

"Humans?" Mia asked.

"Nah. There aren't any clean cuts. This was teeth and claws, not knives."

Mia grinned. "I hope we don't have a feral children problem."

"The only thing I can think of is that some wolves took it down, and then some other wolves came along and tried to claim the kill. During the fight, the deer got ripped up all over the place."

"Wouldn't one group of wolves have won, though?"

"Yeah, probably."

"If it was such a big fight that the deer got strewn

around like this, we'd see some evidence, right? Maybe not a whole dead wolf, but there'd be fur. I don't see anything." Mia walked over to the edge of the creek. "There aren't any bites taken out of the lower half."

"See, how do you know I'm not keeping you from a career as a crime scene investigator?"

Mia went around the area, carefully looking at each of the many, many pieces of deer. Rusty wasn't sure what he was supposed to be looking for, so he just watched her.

"I can't say for sure," said Mia, finally, "but I don't think any of this deer was eaten."

"Really?"

"Maybe they took a bite here and there, but it kind of seems like the whole deer is accounted for. It's just spread all over. It's like the deer was murdered. I know that sounds dumb—let me try to think of how to say it..."

"You're saying that it wasn't killed for food."

"Right."

"Which is the only reason a wild animal would kill another wild animal."

"Right."

"Yeah, that's weird," said Rusty. "Maybe we *do* have feral children running around."

"At least the parts aren't arranged into some freaky pattern, like it was a cult ritual."

"That's a definite upside."

"By the way, if you send me away, there's a very good chance I'll join a cult. Just throwing that out there."

"Noted." Even without a cultish, demon-summoning, Satan-worshipping element, Rusty had to admit that this was creeping him out a little. Also, if fresh deer meat was lying out like this and hadn't been taken away by scavengers, this massacre was still very recent. Which meant that whatever had done it might still be nearby. "We should head back," he said.

"Yeah."

They returned to the cabin, not running but certainly not strolling at the same leisurely pace as before. Giving Mia the opportunity to test out the world beyond their off-the-grid existence was the right choice, but Rusty had to admit right now that it was nice to not be alone.

CHAPTER THREE

Rusty and Mia continued to brainstorm possibilities for what might have happened. Some of their theories were moderately credible, while others were purposely absurd. They laughed a lot, and Rusty got the impression that Mia was much more comfortable talking about the gruesome fate of the deer than her (hopefully) temporary vacation from the cabin.

He was pretty sure that she was just afraid, which meant that it was his responsibility to push her out of her comfort zone to do this. There were thousands of good reasons to stay out here forever, but fear was not one of them. He'd wait for her to bring up the subject again, but if she didn't in, say, a week or so, he'd have to do it.

"What if the deer did it to itself?" Mia asked.

"What?"

"Hear me out. Let's say you're a deer with low self-esteem. Sure, you could drown yourself or jump off a cliff, but if you wanted to really go out in style, you'd tear yourself apart."

"Even in the context of you trying to be as ridiculous

as possible, that doesn't make sense," Rusty informed her.

"Aliens, then."

"It was wolves that got scared away by something. If we went back down there, we'd probably find them finishing up their dinner."

"Have fun. I won't wait up."

"I didn't say I was going."

"Oh, sorry. My mistake. I thought you were in a wolf-fightin' mood."

It was Rusty's turn to make dinner, so he boiled a pot of water on their gas stove for spaghetti. His commitment to living away from society did not include insanity like trying to make his own pasta. He was perfectly content to buy pre-packaged spaghetti, and the hamburger had also been purchased from the store. In many ways he was a hypocrite, but he was okay with that—it wasn't as if he went on angry rants or tried to convince others that his was the only way to live.

The spaghetti was a little undercooked, but Mia assured him that she didn't mind; she'd simply underwash the dishes to balance it out. After everything was cleaned up, they settled in for an evening of reading: Rusty reading an action-packed adventure novel, and Mia reading *Lord of the Flies* as homework. (Her previous reading assignment had been *Wuthering Heights*, which Rusty absolutely hated. He was glad they were past that shit.)

After a couple of hours and several literary machine gun battles, Rusty gave Mia a kiss on the forehead and retired to his bedroom. He climbed into bed, turned off the kerosene lamp, and closed his eyes.

A few minutes later, he was still awake.

This was unusual for him. Rusty was the kind of guy who could fall asleep like flipping off a light switch. If he was stressed out over something, he might lose his appetite, but he'd been blessed with a mind that was happy to put everything on hold until the next morning. Lying in bed, staring at the ceiling, simply wasn't normal behavior for him.

He considered saying, "Screw it," and getting up to read some more, but he didn't want Mia to think anything weird was going on. He'd give it a few more minutes, at least.

It was probably just the double dose of accepting that Mia might not be with him forever and the weird-ass deer massacre. One or the other wouldn't disrupt his sleep, but both of them at once forced his mind to obsess a little bit. He certainly wasn't worried that whatever killed the deer would get into the cabin. There were plenty of bears in the woods, but unless you did something stupid like leaving food out or getting between a mother and her cubs, they weren't going to bother you.

He and Mia were perfectly safe.

Rusty lay there for a few more minutes, wide-awake.

Damn.

He rarely noticed the noises of the forest anymore. After he first moved out here, twenty-five years ago, when he turned out the lights and sat in the darkness it sounded like he was completely surrounded by danger. It was easy to imagine that if he stepped outside of the cabin, glowing-eyed hellhounds with oversized incisors were waiting to pounce. But it was actually an exhilarating kind of fear. Now, he didn't even hear the animals that he knew were out there.

Tonight, he did. Things rustling in the trees. A bird

cawing. A distant howling.

Nothing that could get at them, though. It was stupid to think otherwise.

He did hear a scratching that didn't sound all that far away. He ignored the other noises and tried to focus on it. It wasn't a spooky scratching, like a vampire very slowly scraping its fingernails across a window, but a rapid scratching.

Rusty had no idea what it was. Probably nothing. Definitely nothing. If he paid attention, he was sure he'd be able to hear something like that on any given night.

He decided to try silently counting to clear his mind and let him fall asleep. At six hundred and forty-six, he finally did.

When he woke up, it was still dark and he had to pee.

Of the many downsides to getting older, this was the most annoying. He used to be able to sleep through the night. He'd only be woken with the need to urinate if he'd had a big slice of watermelon right before bed. Now, even if he purposely had nothing to drink for several hours before falling asleep, his body would find some hidden reserve. There were no exceptions.

But at least he woke up instead of wetting the bed, which he assumed was the next exciting phase of the aging process.

He got out of bed and slid his feet into the bright green fuzzy slippers Mia had gotten him for his birthday a couple of years ago. It had been a joke, but damn were they comfortable. He'd definitely get another pair when these wore out.

He stepped out of his bedroom. He'd done an outstanding job on the cabin floor and the wood didn't creak as he walked toward the front door. Despite the much nicer bathroom inside, Rusty remained committed to the outhouse for his middle of the night pee breaks, weather permitting, and no way in hell was he going to disrupt his routine out of fear of a wild animal.

He opened the door. Rusty kept the hinges well oiled, so the process was soundless. If he peed inside, the flush would awaken Mia and she'd want to know what was wrong. Rusty didn't vary his routine very often.

Rusty stepped outside and then hesitated. He could still hear the scratching. In fact, though he couldn't quite pinpoint its location, it seemed to be coming from the outhouse.

It was an admirable trait to not let fear rule one's life, but it was also admirable to not be a complete dumbass. Though technically he could just pee off the side of the porch, he tried not to be a savage unless he was out for a walk by himself. He would urinate indoors tonight.

After he finished, he considered not flushing, but Mia had made it clear that in bad weather she'd rather be woken up than be confronted with an unflushed toilet, "even if it's just number one." He flushed and left the bathroom. Mia, who'd been a light sleeper since she was a baby, emerged from her bedroom.

"Is it raining?" she asked.

"No." Rusty was a little embarrassed, but then he decided there was no reason for it. Mia sure as hell wouldn't be venturing over to the outhouse if she heard scratching near it. "There's something out there."

"A wolf?"

"I don't know." Rusty walked over to the door and opened it. "You hear that?"

Mia stepped into the doorway. "The scratching?"

Rusty felt oddly relieved that she heard it, too, even though there'd been no point where he thought it was ghost-scratching. "What do you think it is?"

"Something that got trapped in the outhouse?"

Rusty nodded. "That makes sense."

"Are you going to let it out?"

"I don't know."

"It could die in there. Why scoop up a dead animal if you don't have to?"

"Yeah, yeah, you're right." Rusty picked up the flashlight that they kept on a shelf next to the door. "Back in a second."

"Let me put on my shoes. I'll come with you."

"You don't have to."

"I want to know what it is. If I shine the flashlight and you open the outhouse door, we can see what runs out."

"All right. Stay on the porch, though."

Mia frowned. "You really think it's something dangerous?"

"No, but you saw the deer."

"Something that got trapped in the outhouse wouldn't be big enough to shred a deer."

"Still, stay on the porch."

"The flashlight beam won't reach that far."

Rusty sighed. "Fine. Get close enough to light up the front of the outhouse, but don't walk right up to it, okay?"

"Okay."

Mia put on the bright rainbow-colored fuzzy slippers that Rusty had bought her as revenge for his birthday

28

present, and they left the cabin.

It was a pretty good flashlight, but the outhouse was about a hundred feet away from the cabin and off to the side. Rusty didn't actually care that much about what was making the scratching sounds as long as it went away, but Mia was right that she couldn't have properly illuminated it without leaving the porch. She was also right that a giant deer-ripping-in-half creature couldn't fit into the outhouse, unless it had been a werewolf who'd now reverted to his human form. It probably wasn't.

Rusty walked toward the outhouse. The scratching was definitely coming from there. And as he got closer, he could also hear some thrashing, and some squeaks.

He stepped up to the door and grabbed the handle. He glanced back at Mia to make sure she'd kept her distance, and then threw the door open.

Nothing came out. The noises continued.

Rusty backed up a few feet, then walked over so that he could see inside the outhouse. As far as he could tell, there was nothing in there, but he was standing in front of the light, so something could be masked by the shadows. He walked back toward Mia. "Let me have the light."

She handed it to him. Rusty returned to the outhouse and shone the light all around the inside, while remaining a safe distance away. No signs of anything in there, though the sounds continued. If it was underneath the toilet seat—well, the poor animal would just have to suffocate.

"I think it's coming from behind it," said Mia.

Rusty listened carefully.

Yep, she was right. It was coming from behind the outhouse.

This did not make him happy.

That said, it was also clear that whatever was behind there was relatively small. It wasn't as if a grizzly bear was going to claw his face off as soon as he shined the flashlight in its eyes. The mangled deer and this were quite clearly unrelated, so there was no reason not to just walk back there and see what it was.

It was a squirrel. It was thrashing around because its front paw was caught in a crack in the wood near the bottom. Had it been trying to dig its way through?

No. That was stupid. Squirrels didn't try to dig through walls. It had been scurrying across the wall and gotten stuck, that's all. Its front leg was in there pretty deep, but it could've gotten wedged in there more tightly while it was trying to escape.

He stepped away from the cabin and called back to Mia. "Just a squirrel."

She hurried over to take a look. "Poor thing."

"Yeah."

"What do we do?"

The harshest option was to inform the squirrel that life was tough, and that sometimes there was nobody to solve your problems for you. Let the squirrel figure out its own solution. This meant that in the morning they'd probably have to remove a dead squirrel, or at least the chewed-off leg of one. Rusty didn't care much about the welfare of the squirrels in the woods, but this seemed rather cruel.

Another option was to put the squirrel out of its misery before it died a lingering death overnight. Grab a plank of plywood and splatter the poor bastard. It wouldn't be the first time Rusty had done a mercy killing of a forest dweller, but this option also held little appeal.

It wasn't as if he'd be haunted, waking up screaming every night with visions of a tiny squirrel head caving in, but still, it would be extremely unpleasant.

Which left trying to free it. This was the most humane, kind-hearted option, the one where he could lay his head on the pillow with a smile on his face at the thought of a job well done. It was also the option where he could get injured by a crazed squirrel. He didn't want to lose an eye to that thing.

"We're gonna get it free," Rusty said.

"You mean pry the wood apart?"

"I was thinking more of just pulling it out of there."

"Do you think it's rabid?"

Rusty aimed the flashlight beam at the creature, looking for signs of foam on its mouth. (Did rabid squirrels foam at the mouth? He wasn't sure. It seemed like something he should know.)

The beam caught its eyes, which were...odd.

"What's wrong with its eyes?" asked Mia.

"I don't know." Squirrels had black beady eyes. This one's eyes weren't *red*, exactly, but they were bloodshot. At least it seemed that way. It was thrashing around too much to be sure.

"I'll go get a blanket," said Mia.

"Make sure it's a thick one," Rusty told her. "And my gloves. And the machete."

"The machete?"

"In case I have to kill it."

"Maybe we should let it die."

"No, no, it'll be fine. Just being extra cautious. And, actually, get two blankets."

While Mia went to retrieve their squirrel-rescuing supplies, Rusty kept trying to get a good look at its eyes.

Bloodshot eyes on a squirrel were damned unnerving, but it made sense that it might have popped a few vessels during its struggle.

"We're going to get you out of there," he informed it. "Just hang in there a little bit longer."

The squirrel continued to freak out. Rusty couldn't say that he blamed it. It was thrashing around a lot more now, as if it knew that Rusty had briefly considered the "splatter it with a plank of wood" option, and if they were lucky it might knock itself unconscious.

Mia returned with the blankets, machete, and his leather work gloves that were hopefully resistant to being punctured by squirrel teeth. Rusty took the gloves from her and put them on.

"What do you want me to do?" she asked.

"Just hold the flashlight on it, and be ready to run if things go wrong."

"I'm not running away from a squirrel."

"You are if it gets loose and goes berserk."

"You will make fun of me literally forever if I run away from a berserk squirrel."

Rusty shook his head. "I won't. I promise."

"Bullshit. If I run back to the cabin and fall on my ass, you'll laugh yourself into a hernia."

"Nobody's asking you to fall on your ass."

"If I'm running away from a psycho rodent, it could happen."

"Seriously, Mia, there could be something wrong with it. If I tell you to run, you run, okay?"

Mia nodded.

Rusty took the machete from her and leaned it against the outhouse, within reach if necessary. He supposed that he could trust Mia to hold it, but in the unlikely event that the squirrel *did* leap out at her he didn't want her flailing around in a panic with a bladed weapon. That was a good way for him to lose an arm or a head.

"All I'm going to do is wrap it in the blanket and pull," he said.

"Try not to tear its arm off."

"I'll be gentle." He took the blankets from her. "Step back."

Mia backed away, keeping the light aimed at the squirrel.

Rusty wondered if this was the dumbest thing he'd ever done. He was, in general, not a guy who was prone to bumbling antics. He wasn't perfect by any stretch of the imagination, but if he went back and reviewed each decision he'd made during the course of his life, he genuinely believed that there would be more marks on the "smart" side than the "jaw-droppingly stupid" side. But now he was about to yank a squirrel out of a crack in his outhouse wall. That might be enough to balance out a couple hundred of his intelligent decisions.

There was no reason to wait any longer. The squirrel wasn't going any less insane.

Rusty got as close as he could without putting himself in claw range, then covered the animal in the blanket. It did not appear to like this. He quickly wrapped it up as tightly as he could, then very gently lifted the bundle.

It didn't come loose.

"Is it coming loose?" Mia asked.

Rusty didn't answer. He wanted to maintain his full concentration on the task at hand. He was grateful to Mia for not laughing; this was the kind of stuff that people living normal lives would record and post online to be ridiculed by millions.

He tugged again, continuing to do it gently.

It still didn't come loose. The squirrel was going absolutely ballistic in there. Rusty was kind of surprised that it hadn't broken its own leg in the struggle. At least it wasn't ripping through the blanket.

He yanked once more, a little harder than the first two times, but hopefully not hard enough to make the squirrel's leg pop off.

It came free.

Rusty immediately set the blanket on the ground. The squirrel continued thrashing around inside of it. Rusty glanced at the outhouse and was relieved to note that there wasn't a bloody squirrel leg wedged in the crack.

He shook out the blanket a bit then stepped out of the way. The lump of the squirrel moved to the edge, then switched direction and moved to the upper right corner. Then it switched direction again and moved back to the center.

He wanted to help it, but he also didn't want to get rabies just to make things a little easier for the squirrel to make its escape. The squirrel moved around underneath the blanket for nearly a minute until finally it emerged, looking unharmed. It scampered up the nearest tree.

"You're welcome, asshole," Rusty called up after it.

"Well, that was interesting," said Mia, walking over to him. "I can't believe you want me to leave and miss that kind of excitement."

"I don't want you to leave."

"I know."

The branches rustled above.

Mia shined the flashlight beam on the back of the outhouse. "If I were a squirrel, and I were trying to dig through a wall, that's not the wall I would choose."

"I don't think it was trying to dig through anything."

"Either way, I hope it's learned a valuable lesson."

The branches rustled again. Mia shined the light up there.

The squirrel leapt out of the tree at them.

Rusty had just enough time to hold up his arm, so the squirrel struck that instead of his head. It scurried up his arm and onto his shoulder. He frantically batted at it with his other hand as the squirrel ran across the back of his neck.

"Holy shit!" said Mia, swinging the flashlight at it.

The squirrel nuzzled its face against Rusty's collar as if trying to get inside of his shirt, then ran halfway down his back. Rusty swatted at it but it was like an itch he couldn't reach.

"Hold still!" Mia told him.

Rusty didn't want to hold still. He hurried over to the outhouse and slammed his back against it, hoping to crush the wretched rodent. Too slow. The squirrel ran around to his chest, and Mia's attempt to smack it with the flashlight missed.

It ran across his arm. He vigorously tried to shake it off, but the squirrel had a firm grip with its claws and wouldn't go anywhere. Then he tried to grab its tail so that he could fling it away. Still no luck. The damn thing was too fast.

Mia struck it with the flashlight. It wasn't a skull-crushing blow, though; it hit the squirrel on the side but seemed to have no effect on its behavior.

The squirrel bit down on Rusty's index finger. It hurt, but thank God he was wearing the gloves. He still couldn't shake it off. He tried to clap his hands together but it scurried back up his arm and across the back of his neck again.

He desperately hoped he didn't get bit in a way that broke the skin. As long as he didn't catch a disease, they'd be able to look back on this and laugh. They wouldn't be laughing if he were rabid.

"Stop moving," Mia told him. "I mean it, stop moving."

Rusty realized that she was now holding the machete. He stopped moving.

Mia lunged with the weapon and missed. She lunged again, and the squirrel let out a high-pitched, agonized shriek. She swung the machete out of the way, and Rusty turned around to see the still-thrashing squirrel skewered on it.

She slammed the blade into the dirt, deep enough for it to stand up on its own. They watched as the squirrel slowly slid down, moving less and less frantically, and finally reached the ground.

"That," Mia said, "was fucked up."

Rusty couldn't catch his breath yet, so he just nodded.

The squirrel slowly reached its front leg out at them, as if making a final dying effort to attack its prey, and then went still.

Mia pulled the machete out. They both spent a long moment just staring at its dead body.

"I don't think we'll be throwing that one on the grill," said Mia.

Rusty still wasn't recovered enough to acknowledge her witticism. He took off the gloves and ran his fingers over the back of his neck.

"Here, let me check," Mia said. She looked him over. "The scratches aren't bad. Do they hurt?"

"No, not really. I was lucky."

"What was wrong with that thing?"

"I have no idea. It was scratching for quite a while. Maybe it was so panicked from the experience that it went mentally ill."

"Aren't all squirrels mentally ill?"

"That wasn't a scientific theory. I really don't know what happened. I've gotta say, I was happier with the outcome before you had to impale that thing with a machete."

"Me too." Mia looked at the machete blade. "That's really weird."

"What?"

She leaned the machete against the outhouse and shined the flashlight on it. She ran the beam up the length of the blade.

"That *is* weird," said Rusty.

There were traces of brown fur and skin on the machete, but absolutely no blood.

CHAPTER FOUR

They went back to the cabin and got a plastic bag. When they returned to the outhouse, the dead squirrel was still where they'd left it, which should not have been a surprise. Rusty didn't want to pick it up, even with gloved hands, or even move it with his foot, so he held the bag open while Mia pushed it in there with the machete. It would've been easier to just stab it, like somebody picking up litter in a park, but that seemed oddly disrespectful, even though the squirrel already had a hole in it.

Rusty tied up the bag and tried to decide where to store the squirrel. Sometime—not necessarily tomorrow, but soon—he'd take it into town and track down a veterinarian to satisfy his curiosity about what was wrong with it. It had to be some kind of disease that would make it act that way and also coagulate its blood so thick that it didn't spill out when it was stabbed. Rusty had never heard of this sort of thing. Though he was no biologist, he was pretty sure that mammals needed their blood to circulate for them to stay alive.

He didn't want it inside the cabin. And he didn't want it adding a dead animal smell to the already unfragrant outhouse. Other wild animals probably wouldn't dig a dead squirrel out of a garbage bag, so he tossed it into the back of his pickup truck.

This was one of the very rare times that Rusty wished he had more technology at his fingertips. He had a pretty large selection of books in the cabin, but nothing that would provide research material on squirrel diseases. A vet might say, "Oh, yeah, Mad Squirrel Disease. It's all over the news. Where have you been?"

He also wished he drank alcohol. He could use a beer.

He'd settle for a shower. "Do you want to get in there first?" he asked Mia after they were back in the cabin. "Because I'm going to use up all of the hot water."

"It's all yours," she said. "You've earned it."

Rusty didn't realize how much he'd been perspiring until his shirt stuck to him while he peeled it off. Pre-teenaged Mia, he'd had a small hot water tank and went with quick, efficient, no-frills showers, but now they had a huge tank and it was rare for a shower to end just because the water was cold. He stood under the wonderfully refreshing spray, thankful to be here instead of outside fighting that goddamn squirrel.

As he squirted the shampoo into his palm, he realized that his hands were quivering.

Okay, that was stupid. Yes, it had been a bizarre encounter, but still, it was just a squirrel. It hadn't clawed his eyes out. The bite hadn't punctured his skin. He hadn't almost died. Rusty was a man of nature, and squirrels were pretty low on the list of threats. Thinking, "Wow, that was messed up!" was acceptable. Treating it like post-traumatic stress disorder was not.

He washed his hair, lathered himself up with a bar of soap, rinsed himself off, and then stood under the water with his eyes closed. It felt wonderful. Perhaps his anxiety didn't simply wash away, but he did grow less and less tense, and by the time the water transitioned from hot to lukewarm he was feeling relatively back to normal.

He'd assumed that Mia would've gone to bed, but when he emerged from the bathroom she was still awake. She was sitting on the couch in the living room. She didn't have a book or anything, so apparently she'd just been sitting there, waiting.

"You should get some sleep," he told her.

"Just wanted to make sure you were okay."

"I'm totally fine."

"When do we get to laugh about it?"

"Four o'clock tomorrow afternoon."

Mia got up off the couch, walked over, and gave him a tight hug. Mia was a hugger, but they didn't usually linger like this.

"I'm fine!" Rusty insisted. "It was a stupid squirrel! A rat with a bushy tail!"

"Calling it a rat with a bushy tail doesn't help," she said, releasing the hug.

"It's not a big deal at all. It's an amusing anecdote for the next time we go into town. Nothing for either of us to be concerned about. An unusual occurrence, that's all."

"Along with the dead deer," said Mia.

"Okay, yes, the dead deer is also an unusual occurrence."

"On the same day."

"Yes, we've had two very strange animal-related incidents on the same day. I won't lose my shit if you don't."

"They have to be connected, don't they?"

"Not necessarily," said Rusty, although it was one hell of a coincidence to have two completely out of the ordinary things like this happen so close together. "I don't care how psycho that squirrel was, and I don't care how many of them were working in a group, they couldn't tear a deer in half."

"Maybe it's not just squirrels," said Mia.

Rusty wished she hadn't expressed that thought out loud. Now they had no choice but to confront the possibility, instead of simply dismissing it as ridiculous. It *was* ridiculous, but so was a squirrel that didn't bleed when you impaled it with a machete.

"You know what," said Rusty, "it's better to be overly cautious and be embarrassed by it later than to die in a really stupid way. So from now on, neither of us goes outside alone. That includes me. I'm not trying to be a hero. And if we do go out, it's only during the daytime. Just until we get this figured out. And, actually, we don't need to worry about only going out in the daytime because we'll take the squirrel corpse into town first thing tomorrow morning, so we'll have it figured out before we have to worry about going outside in the dark. Sound like a plan?"

"Works for me."

"Good. Everything's going to be fine." He gave her a hug. "Now we need to get some sleep. If you want, I'll sleep on the couch and you can drag your mattress out here."

Mia grinned. "I'm not scared. Weirded out, but not scared." The grin faded. "Though I guess we could at least keep our doors open."

This time, Rusty had to count to seven hundred and thirty to fall asleep, though he did start over when he realized he was counting rabid squirrels.

He woke up at sunrise, as usual. Rusty almost never remembered his dreams (and when he did, they were of the "Oh no, it's finals week and I haven't been to class all semester!" variety), but he felt like he'd been plagued by horrific nightmares. He sure hoped he hadn't whimpered or screamed in his sleep.

He wanted to go out and check on the squirrel, to see if maybe it had bled overnight. Of course, he couldn't do that right after making the rule that they didn't go outside alone. The truck was only parked about fifty feet away, so not being able to walk over to it in daylight was silly, but rules were rules. Though he rarely had to play the role of disciplinarian, and Mia was practically an adult now, he still didn't want to set a poor precedent.

He read for about an hour, having difficulty focusing on the words, until Mia got up.

"Good morning, Sunshine!" he said.

Mia muttered something incoherent and unpleasant. She wasn't a morning person even when her sleep wasn't interrupted by insane wildlife. Rusty had taken her home schooling extremely seriously and made her work hard, but he'd quickly learned that it was much more pleasant to let her set her own hours.

"I'm going to check on the squirrel," he told her.

"Why? You think it might not be dead anymore?"

"Smartass. I want to see if there's any blood in the bag now."

"So you think it could've just been a slow bleeder?"

"I don't know. Maybe. That sounds dumb, but can you think of any explanation that *doesn't* sound dumb?"

"Nope," said Mia. "All I can come up with is zombie squirrel, and that's dumber than slow-bleeding squirrel."

"Let's go check on it."

"Can I make some coffee first?"

"No."

Mia muttered something less coherent and less pleasant as she put on her shoes. They walked out onto the front porch. Rusty had thought about grabbing his rifle before they went out there, but he didn't want to foster more of an environment of paranoia than necessary.

Some birds were chirping. The sounds of nature seemed normal.

They looked into the back of the truck.

"Uhhh..." said Mia.

There was just a shredded garbage bag. No sign of the dead squirrel.

"I'm going to run back and get the broom," Rusty said. "Don't touch anything."

"I totally guarantee you that I won't."

Rusty hurried back to the cabin, unsure why his heart was racing. A dead animal getting eaten by a live animal was the way things worked in nature. Maybe less often when they were tied up in garbage bags in the back of a pickup truck, but still, it wasn't as if the squirrel had disappeared without a trace.

He took the broom out of the closet then returned to the truck. He climbed up into the back and then used the broom handle to move the pieces of garbage bag around. There were bits of fur, but no blood and no bones. Whatever got to the squirrel had either taken it away or devoured the entire thing.

"What would eat a dead squirrel like that?" Mia asked.

"Lots of things."

"Bugs, maybe, but they'd leave remnants. Birds wouldn't swoop down, tear open the bag, and carry the squirrel away. There's no animal that would just climb in the back of your truck and do this."

"Well, clearly there is," said Rusty.

"You don't think it's weird?"

"Yeah, I think it's weird! I think it's beyond weird. I'll even say that it's creepy and upsetting. But I know I didn't take it, and I know you didn't take it—you didn't take it, right? So we're left with two possibilities: an animal got rid of it, or it climbed out of my truck on its own." Rusty furrowed his brow, stroked his chin, and pretended to weigh the alternatives. "I don't know, I'm not God or anything, but I'm relatively certain that the dead squirrel didn't leave on its own."

"Are we sure it was dead?" Mia asked.

"Was it an optical illusion that you stuck a machete right through its torso?"

"I'm just saying, we didn't chop off its head or do a thorough medical examination of it."

"You turned it into a shish kabob."

"Maybe I missed the vital organs."

"Are you hearing yourself?"

Mia sighed. "Uncle Rusty, I've been here for every step

of this. I know how it sounds."

"Well, I'm way more inclined to believe that a wolf jumped up in here and ate it than that the squirrel woke up and left."

"All right, that's reasonable. I guess it doesn't matter now anyway. Are we still going into town?"

Rusty thought about that. Without bringing a dead animal to examine, he and Mia were left with sharing a story that sounded like something you'd make up to play a joke on a gullible veterinarian. He didn't want to travel all that way just to tell a story that completely lacked credibility. "Nah," he said. "We'll wait until we have to murder another one."

"That's a good idea," said Mia. "Because after you told the story, I was going to pretend like I had no idea what you were talking about. Let them cart you away. Inherit the cabin early."

Rusty smiled. "It's scary how much you remind me of your mother."

After breakfast, they got to work. Rusty and Mia had very different processes. Unless he was using a large tool like the table saw, Rusty liked to work on the front porch. He liked to show off his creations each step of the way, describing to Mia exactly what he was doing and what he planned to do. Mia, on the other hand, didn't like Rusty to see her projects until they were completely done. Not to the point where she'd throw a cloth over them if Rusty came into the shed to use some tools, but she'd glare at him if his gaze lingered on her work. Rusty supposed this was a byproduct of him being overzealous with his advice while she was still learning the trade. Though she did ask for assistance if she truly needed it, for the most part she built her furniture completely on her own. And while he couldn't honestly say that her craftsmanship rivaled his own, she was getting there.

Usually he could completely lose himself in his work, become so immersed that Mia had learned to make eye contact before telling him it was time for lunch to avoid startling him. Today he kept thinking about squirrels.

There were squirrels all over the place. He saw them all day, every day. They were such a constant presence in his life that he was barely aware of their existence. Now, every time he heard a squirrel scurry across a branch he wondered if this one might also leap down upon him. (The porch was covered, so the only way one could leap down upon him was if it was a flying squirrel, but that wasn't sufficient consolation.) Each rustling of leaves, even those caused by the wind and not wildlife, made him tense up a bit, as if there might be a reprise of last night. If he worked back in the shed with Mia he'd be free of even the irrational concern that a flying squirrel might get him, but he'd be damned if he was going to hide away like that. If he wanted restrictions on his freedom, he could go back to live in the civilized world.

Damn, there were a lot of squirrels around here.

Furry little creeps.

Rotten nut-burying little shits.

Their chatter, which he'd always been able to tune out, was really getting on his nerves. Like they were laughing at him.

Oh well. Better that they were laughing at him than pissed off at what he'd done to their sibling. He didn't need thousands of squirrels dropping from the trees and charging at him *en masse.*

He really needed to get over this. Yes, last night had been upsetting, but a fifty-year-old man who'd spent half of his life living in the woods should not be trembling in fear over the thought of vengeful squirrels. He needed to suck it up. Odd things happened in the world, and you couldn't let them scare you. At least not once the danger was over.

Rusty made a conscious effort to focus on his work.

After a couple of hours, the effort was no longer conscious. He was back to being able to tune out those wretched creatures while sanding down some table legs. It was soothing work. Even a little hypnotic.

They had ham sandwiches and potato chips for lunch. They did not speak of squirrels.

By late afternoon, Rusty was amused by the whole thing. If he was the kind of person to speak to a therapist (and there was no conceivable scenario where he would be) they'd be too busy laughing to get any psychoanalysis done.

He'd forgotten about squirrels altogether until he saw a familiar figure slowly crawling toward him.

CHAPTER FIVE

Rusty knew he wasn't hallucinating.

Nor was he mistaking what he was seeing. Various parts of his body were no longer operating at the efficiency of his youth, but his eyes were still fine. Perhaps it wasn't the *same* squirrel (they all pretty much looked identical) but there was most definitely an injured squirrel crawling toward the front porch of his cabin.

He stood up and stepped off the porch, not looking away from the animal. Though it was moving too slowly to pose a threat, it was headed straight for him. It lifted its head and let out a soft but angry squeal.

"Mia!" Rusty called out. "Hey, Mia!"

If she was in the shed with the door closed while sanding wood she might not hear him. It would only take a moment to go get her, but he didn't want to leave the squirrel. He walked over to it—closer, but not *close*—and, yeah, the machete wound was there. Not that there'd been any real doubt, but it was the same freaking squirrel.

The most appealing course of action was to stomp on

the unholy abomination a few times. Unfortunately, if he was going to get answers, he had to keep it alive.

The squirrel looked at him with its bloodshot eyes. Though it was difficult to gauge homicidal intent in the gaze of a squirrel, this thing really did give the impression of wanting to kill him.

"Mia! Get the hell out here!"

The squirrel was now about six feet away from him. That was too close. Rusty took a step back.

Nobody was going to believe this. Nobody *should* believe this. Only the most gullible idiot would believe an anecdote about what was happening right here.

On some level, he had to admire the creature's determination. If Rusty had a machete blade go right through him, he'd abandon whatever task he was trying to complete. He felt bad that the squirrel was going through hell on earth to get to him, yet would be denied even a single bite of its chosen prey.

He called Mia's name again, stretching it out as long as possible. The squirrel would surely still be here after he went to get her, but he didn't want to risk it. He didn't even want to risk looking away long enough to grab something with which to trap it.

Mia hurried around the side of the cabin. Before she could ask him what was wrong, she saw it. "Is that the same—?"

"Yes."

"Holy fuck."

"Yeah."

"I don't even *want* to know what's going on with it," said Mia. "It's nothing good. Do you want me to get you a block of wood to drop on it?"

"No," said Rusty. "I do want to know what's wrong

with it."

"Something demonic."

"It's not..." Rusty didn't finish his sentence. He didn't have enough information right now to rule out the idea that it was a demon squirrel crawling toward him. "We're not going to crush it. Get me something to put it in."

"A bowl of holy water?"

"Something to put over it." Rusty had to take another step back. He was curious as to just how devoted this thing was to getting at him. If he went back onto the porch, would it try to get up the two stairs?

Mia went into the cabin. She returned a moment later with the large pot he'd used to make spaghetti. "You can trap it in this, or you can use it to flatten it. I'd use it to flatten it."

Rusty took the pot from her. "Don't we have a box or something?"

"Have you made a box lately?"

He approached the squirrel. He was fairly certain that he could slam the upside-down pot over it without getting injured, but "fairly certain" was not the same as "one hundred percent certain." He'd toss it instead. He crouched down, took careful aim, and then tossed the pot, which successfully landed over the squirrel, not even pinching its tail.

Clang! Clang! Clang!

"He's pissed," said Mia.

The clanging continued.

"I mean, he's *really* pissed."

"You would be too," said Rusty. "Make sure it doesn't go anywhere. I'll be back in a second."

"Where are you going?"

"You didn't get me a lid, or any way to turn the pot

over without letting it go."

"Oh. Yeah, I guess I didn't think it through because I was so distracted by the zombie squirrel. I'll go get it. You babysit your new pet." Mia went back inside.

The clanging was really intense. That thing had an amazing amount of energy left. Did squirrels have adrenaline?

Clang! Clang! Clang! Clang! Clang!

Mia came out with the lid to the pot and a metal cookie sheet. "You can slide this underneath it," she said, stepping off the porch and handing the sheet to him.

The clanging stopped. Rusty set the cookie sheet on the ground, next to the edge of the pot.

"Do you need help?" Mia asked.

"Nah, I've got this."

Mia crouched down next to the pot and placed her hands on the top. "I'll keep it from moving. But if that thing gets out, I'm jumping right in the truck and starting my two-week vacation now."

"If it gets out, I'll come with you." Rusty took a deep breath, gathering his courage for a task that really should not have required courage. "I have to lift the pot a tiny bit." He raised it just enough to get the cookie sheet underneath it, then slowly slid the sheet underneath the entire pot. The squirrel didn't seem to be moving anymore.

"That wasn't so hard," said Mia. "On the count of three, we'll flip it over."

They counted to three, and flipped the pot over while keeping the cookie sheet pressed against it. No incident. There was a *thunk* as the squirrel dropped to the bottom.

"I don't think it's going to leap out at us," said Rusty. "In fact, I'm positive it won't. But move back anyway."

Mia, without protest, stood up and took several steps backward.

Rusty quickly swapped the cookie sheet with the glass lid. The squirrel did not leap out at him. It would not be doing any more leaping. Rusty grimaced.

Mia returned to the pot and peered inside. "Oh my God..."

The squirrel had bashed itself into mush. There was still clear evidence that it was a squirrel, like the fuzzy tail, but little remained of its head and the left side of its body was severely mangled. Still no blood; plenty of brain matter, intestines, and other assorted innards. Its bloodshot eyes had both burst, assuming that Rusty was indeed looking at its eyes in the sludge.

"How did it even do that to itself?" Rusty asked.

"It must have really wanted out of that pot."

"Look at it. You don't smush up your head like that with one smack against a metal pot. It kept going after its skull was broken and its brains were leaking out. *You* could splatter my head like that, if you were really mad at me, but I couldn't do it to myself."

"Zombie squirrel?"

"I mean, your body twitches and stuff after you're dead. If it got some momentum going, I guess it's possible that it killed itself with one really vicious bash against the metal and then it was muscle spasms that did the rest, but it would have to *really* hit that thing hard to do this kind of damage."

"So...zombie squirrel?"

"I'm not ready to go 'zombie squirrel' quite yet."

"What's your diagnosis, then?" Mia asked.

"I'm going with 'We don't have the expertise to say with any kind of authority what exactly the hell is wrong with that fucked-up squirrel.' We'll let somebody else take a look at it. Let's go."

The first part of the drive into town involved fourteen and a half miles on a dirt road that seemed to have been designed by sadists who hated travelers. Rusty knew where the gigantic potholes were and instinctively avoided them, but if you weren't in that natural rhythm, you had to drive very slowly and stay very alert. There were parts where it was easy to get stuck in the dirt if you didn't know to give your vehicle that extra boost of gas at the right moment. There were parts where the road was just loose jagged rocks. On occasion he'd have to move a fallen tree out of the road; nobody else was doing maintenance because nobody else used the road. There was a brutal hill. The road *sucked.* And Rusty liked it that way.

After finally making it to the paved road, it was then a simple twenty-three mile drive to the nearest town, which was barely a town. And Rusty liked it that way, too.

Mia had become an expert on navigating the unfriendly road. She'd been driving the truck since she was twelve. Rusty assumed at some point that he'd have to get her an official driver's license.

He was driving this time, though. The pot was resting on the seat between them. Rusty wished he could say that its close proximity didn't make him nervous, but that would be a lie. If he weren't concerned about it toppling over and spilling, he would've put it in the back of the truck.

After a couple of miles, he regretted the decision not to transfer the squirrel to something besides a spaghetti pot. They were going to look like squirrel soup-eating hillbillies when they brought this into the veterinarian's office. Maybe they'd buy a more appropriate container after they reached civilization.

The drive was uneventful. There was one fallen tree that was thin enough that Rusty probably could've driven over it without a problem, but they got out and moved it just to be safe. They listened to the '50s station on the radio after getting within signal distance (Mia was going to be gobsmacked by how much other music was available in the world) until they arrived in Clovisville. Rusty pulled into the parking lot of the grocery store and shut off the engine.

Clovisville was too small to have a veterinarian's office, of course. They'd have to make the *extremely* rare trip to Danners (where they went for rare doctor's appointments and even rarer dentist appointments—Rusty and Mia made it a point to take really good care of their teeth), but he needed an address.

Rusty hated cell phones. In the days before them, he could've simply found a pay phone, looked through the Yellow Pages, and found what he needed. Now there were no pay phones in Clovisville, meaning he'd be forced to talk to somebody.

"Hello, Mr. Moss," said Jake, one of the cashiers. He was a good kid who occasionally flirted unsuccessfully with Mia. "Didn't expect to see you back so soon."

"I'm looking for a vet."

"Army vet?"

"Cat and dog vet."

"We take Duchess to Dr. Teal. He runs a private practice out of his house. He's, like, a mile from here, if that."

"That's great," said Rusty. Danners was eighty miles away, and even if it were only eight, not having to go there would make him extremely happy.

"He doesn't have regular hours—just appointments. I could pull up his number and see if he's available now."

"I'd really appreciate that."

"What kind of pet do you have? I've never seen you buy dog or cat food."

Rusty did not feel that this was a situation where he needed to share all of the information. "I've got a biology question." He hoped Jake wouldn't push him for more details.

Jake took out his cell phone and tapped away at the screen for a few moments. He made a call, briefly spoke with somebody, then smiled. "You're all set," he told Rusty. He wrote an address down on a slip of paper and handed it to him.

"Thank you," said Rusty.

"How's everything going with you guys?" Jake asked, directing the question more at Mia than Rusty.

"It's going great," said Mia. "Thanks so much for your help." Her tone was genuinely friendly, not dismissive, but she walked away from the register. Rusty wasn't sure if she had no interest, or if her lack of social interactions meant that she was simply clueless.

Rusty thanked Jake again, and they left the store, hopefully to get some answers.

Dr. Teal's office was just a regular house with a small sign out front. After ringing the doorbell, they were greeted by a heavyset man who looked about thirty. He wore blue jeans and was buttoning a white lab coat.

"Welcome," he said, shaking Mia's hand. Rusty didn't want to let go of the cooking pot, so he didn't offer his hand. "Right this way." The vet led them into a back room, which looked just like any veterinarian's office Rusty had ever been in. There was a scale, a metal table, lots of medical equipment, and posters of cute animals saying amusing things.

"Thanks for seeing us on such short notice," said Rusty.

"No problem at all. What can I do for you?"

Rusty cleared his throat. "This is going to sound strange."

"I'm listening."

"There was this squirrel..."

"Okay, hold on, let me stop you right there," said Dr. Teal. "You may be looking for somebody completely different. I handle domesticated pets. If you're looking for a wildlife expert, I'm not your guy."

"I get that," said Rusty. "I was just hoping you'd hear me out. You might have *some* insight."

"Is there a squirrel in that pot?"

"Yes, sir."

Dr. Teal sighed. "Go on."

Rusty wasn't sure if he should tell the complete version of the saga, or leave out the parts that would make him sound like a madman. He decided that he might as well tell the entire story. Dr. Teal looked more and more annoyed as he went on.

"Mia can confirm all of this," said Rusty, when he was finished.

"Good. I'm glad to hear that the girl you came here with can back you up. I guess I might as well take a look at it."

Dr. Teal took the pot from Rusty, set it on the table, and removed the lid. He stared into it for a few seconds, then replaced the lid.

"Well?" asked Rusty.

"You bashed a squirrel's brains out, then brought it here for me to inspect."

"No."

"It didn't do this to itself. Any fool can see that."

"I know it doesn't seem physically possible—"

"Because it isn't."

"That's why I had all of those disclaimers while I was telling you what happened. I completely understand that this seems impossible."

"You're confusing *seems* impossible with *is* impossible."

"No, it *seems* impossible, because I was there when it happened."

"I was not there," said Dr. Teal. "All I can go by is the evidence in front of me. I'm not sure if you're playing a prank or if magic mushrooms were involved, but what you're telling me happened is not what happened."

The vet's condescending attitude was pissing Rusty off, even though he knew he deserved this attitude because his story was completely absurd.

"Could you at least check out the lack of blood?" Mia asked.

The vet took a penlight out of his pocket, removed the lid again, shined the light down in there, then replaced the lid. "I don't see any blood. Which leads me to believe that instead of hallucinating, you're lying."

"Look at me," said Rusty. "Do I look like somebody who would walk in here and make this stuff up?"

"Liars come in all shapes and sizes."

"What would we have to gain?"

"Amusement. Winning a bet. Attention that you desperately crave but aren't getting elsewhere."

Rusty wanted to tell Dr. Teal to go fuck himself, but he'd been kind enough to see them in the first place and that would be going too far. "Okay, I agree with what you said before, you're not the right guy for this. Can you recommend somebody else?"

"You're asking me to contact one of my professional colleagues and send you over there with a pot of mashed squirrel?"

"They could run some tests. Prove that I'm lying."

"I'm sure you can find somebody who will run some tests on your pet if you pay them. The recommendation won't come from me."

Rusty almost hoped that the squirrel would spring back to life and attack him. Almost. Not quite.

"All right," said Rusty. "I won't try to change your mind."

"If you leave now I won't charge you for this office visit."

Rusty picked up the pot. Dr. Teal escorted them to the front door, waved them out, then shut the door without another word.

"Asshole," said Rusty as they walked toward the truck. "That's why I don't like people. He didn't have to act like that. Why not be respectful? Would that have been so difficult?"

"Should we let Jake know that his vet might be mad at him?" Mia asked.

CHAPTER SIX

One rude small-town veterinarian who worked out of his home was far from their only possible source of information, but to be completely honest, Rusty no longer cared about the squirrel. He just wanted to go back to the cabin. If somebody else treated him this way—and they probably would—he might do something he regretted. At least, something he regretted doing in front of Mia when he was supposed to be setting a good example.

"Where next?" asked Mia, as they drove away.

"Home."

"That's it? We're quitting already?"

"If you want to come back tomorrow and wave the dead squirrel in people's faces, you're more than welcome, but I'm done. We shouldn't have come out here in the first place. What were they ever going to tell us?"

"All right," said Mia. "If you're done, I'm done. Do you want to go back and shove the squirrel guts in the vet's mailbox?"

"Yes. But we're not going to."

After about ten miles on the paved road, it began to pour. Rusty cursed and muttered under his breath.

"What did you say?" Mia asked.

"Nothing."

"Did you say that this is why you hate going into town?"

"Yeah."

"You do know that it rains up at the cabin, right? Rain isn't limited to the civilized world."

"I meant that I hate driving in the rain."

"I'm pretty sure that's not what you meant."

"Fine," said Rusty. "I was being irrational. Completely irrational. Are you happy now?"

"I'm happy that you admitted it, yes."

Rusty clenched the steering wheel more tightly. He knew that he was being completely irrational and didn't care. It would've been *insane* for Dr. Teal to hear his story and not think he was being conned. He should've known before they even scooped the squirrel into a pot that it would take several attempts to find somebody who would spend their valuable time poking around in its remains to determine how it could continue to splatter itself after its brain was exposed. His behavior wasn't logical. He'd never try to convince anybody—including himself—otherwise.

By the time they reached the road that went through the forest, he was feeling less pissy about the whole thing. Though he wasn't ready to laugh about it quite yet, he was no longer seething with rage. The rain hadn't ceased so the road was going to be a bitch to navigate, but the truck was designed for this kind of thing and he wasn't in the mood to wait it out.

After going around the first curve, Rusty put the truck into park.

"What's wrong?" Mia asked.

"Not a thing." He picked up the pot, opened the door, and got out of the truck. He removed the lid, then swung the pot, flinging the squirrel off into some brush. He held up the pot, gathering some rain, then swished it around to clean up the remnants, which he poured onto the road. He replaced the lid, set the pot in the back of the truck, and got back inside.

"You could have waited until it wasn't raining," Mia noted.

"I know."

"Whatever makes you happy, I guess."

"I can't lie. That made me happy." He put the truck back into drive and they continued on their way. The mystery of the psycho squirrel would never be resolved, but Rusty didn't think that his life would be poorer for it.

The road was crap but it was nothing Rusty hadn't handled before. He found having to maintain close focus on what he was doing very soothing—which, yes, also made no sense. The paved road should've been the soothing one. He didn't care.

The deer that leapt out in front of him did it at the worst possible spot. For Rusty, not for the deer itself, which survived unharmed. Deer had a tendency to bound across the path with no notice, but usually it was a "slam the brakes" solution instead of a "swerve" one. But this particular deer appeared when they were on a downward slope, and so Rusty swerved instead of braked. Missed the deer completely. The truck went off the path.

They stopped quickly, without smashing into anything or damaging the vehicle.

"Are you okay?" Rusty asked.

Mia nodded. "Frickin' deer."

Rusty put the truck into reverse and applied the gas. The wheels shot muddy water high up into the air behind it but it didn't move. "Wonderful. Great."

"We've got it out before."

"Yeah." Rusty sighed.

"The squirrel planned this."

"Shut up."

"I can't tell if that was an annoyed 'shut up' or an amused 'shut up.'"

"Both. Do you want to get out now, or wait out the rain?"

"Wait it out. It'll clear up soon."

It did not clear up soon. They sat in the truck for two hours, alternating between silence and word games, until the rain finally thinned to a mist.

Rusty started the engine again and pressed the gas pedal. Same result as before.

"Slide on over," he told Mia, as he opened the door.

"Should we even bother?" Mia asked. "Why not just walk home, wait for the mud to firm up, and come back with boards?"

She was probably right. Rusty *might* be able to push the truck out of the mess, but most likely he'd just get himself drenched in mud and be in an even fouler mood during the three-mile walk home. Best to save this until tomorrow morning.

They dug the umbrellas out from under the seat, got out of the truck, and walked down the muddy path.

"What a waste of a day," said Rusty. "So much stuff we could've gotten done. That cabinet was almost finished, but no, I had to humiliate myself. Watch, we'll probably drag those boards all the way back here and still not be able to get the truck free."

"We'll be able to get the truck free," said Mia.

"Yeah, yeah, we will, I know. It'll be fine. I should've left that rodent to die in the outhouse."

"That would've been heartless."

"Heartless but smarter."

"You're not a cruel person."

"Just let me question my choices, okay?"

At least the weather was kind to them on the walk back, never raining quite enough for them to need to open the umbrellas. Rusty wanted to angrily stomp through some of the mud puddles, but didn't want to behave like a bratty little kid.

They saw plenty of squirrels, which all seemed normal, and plenty of birds, which also all seemed normal, and another deer, about fifty feet back into the woods. It sprinted away as they walked past.

"What's your plan for the rest of the day?" asked Mia as they arrived back at the cabin.

Rusty wanted to sit on the front porch and sulk, but that was not a good answer. "I was going to get back to work. Make up for the lost time today."

"Sounds good to me."

Mia went back to the shed, while Rusty returned to his woodworking on the porch. He was particularly proud of this cabinet, which was almost done except for the varnish and paint, and he found himself getting closer and closer to being amused by what had happened. He didn't think he'd ever quite reach the tipping point, but he conceded that he might reach a state where Mia's amusement didn't irritate him.

When it was time to quit for the day, they went inside

and had a lackluster dinner. Then it started raining again, followed by lightning and thunder. The cabin hadn't leaked since the second year he'd lived there (during the first year, it leaked in a different spot with each storm), so they just relaxed and read for a short while. Then, because he'd gotten so little sleep the previous night, Rusty went to bed early.

He fell asleep immediately.

Then he woke up. It was still raining, though the thunderstorm seemed to have passed.

He heard scraping noises again.

Not over by the outhouse. Something was scraping against the outside wall of the cabin.

And from the sound of it, the source was something *much* bigger than a squirrel.

Rusty got out of bed. The scraping stopped as he walked over to his window. He peered through the glass and saw nothing in the darkness outside.

He hoped he'd imagined it. He probably hadn't.

He left his bedroom and went into the living room. He turned on the outside light. Rusty went from room to room, looking through all of the windows except Mia's, and didn't see anything.

Best to just ignore it, then.

He heard the scraping again. He hurried back into his bedroom. Looked through the window. Nothing in front of it. Nothing to the right. When he looked to the left, he thought he caught a glimpse of something, but it moved around the corner.

He was *not* in the mood for this right now. He needed one peaceful night before he had to deal with this kind of crap again.

Should he wake up Mia?

No. If he decided that he actually needed to go outside to investigate, he'd wake her up, but for now he'd let her sleep.

His palms were sweating. He couldn't deny it: he was legitimately scared.

More scraping. This time it came from the living room. Or at least he thought it did. He went back in there, looked through the window, and saw nothing.

Did he just hear a growl?

He may very well have heard a growl.

He stayed completely still and listened carefully. There wasn't another growl, at least not one he could hear over the rain.

Okay, he needed to stay calm. This was nothing he couldn't handle. He had several guns and plenty of ammunition. If whatever was out there tried to get inside—which it wouldn't—a shotgun blast to the face would take care of that problem.

He did another check of the windows. Nothing.

Then he sat down on the couch, listening for anything unusual.

It was quiet except for the rain.

"Uncle Rusty?"

Rusty flinched at the sound of Mia's voice. She was right in front of him. How had she gotten there without him noticing?

"Why are you sleeping on the couch?" she asked.

He'd fallen asleep. Of course. Made sense.

"I heard something outside," he said. It was still dark. It had either stopped raining or was raining very lightly— he couldn't tell.

"What?"

"Scraping against the sides of the cabin. Maybe a

growl."

Mia frowned. "Did you see what it was?"

Rusty shook his head. "I couldn't see anything through the windows. I'm going to look now."

"Be careful."

Rusty got up off the couch and went over to the cabinet where they kept the guns. He'd stopped locking it on Mia's thirteenth birthday. He wanted one hand free, so he selected the pistol. It was already loaded.

Mia grabbed her rifle. Rusty didn't stop her.

He did another window check, including the one in Mia's room, and saw nothing. Whatever was out there was probably long gone, but maybe it had left clues to what it was, like footprints or a great big pile of scat. Rusty picked up the flashlight, turned it on, walked over to the front door, opened it, and stepped out onto the front porch.

If there'd been muddy footprints, the rain had washed them away. He waved the flashlight beam past where the outside lights would carry, and saw nothing.

"Oh my God," said Mia.

Rusty turned around to see what she was looking at. There was a long scrape across the front wall of the cabin, as if something had raked its claws across the wood for several feet.

"A bear?" Mia asked.

"Looks like it."

"We didn't leave any food out, did we?"

"No." One mistake Rusty had never made in his entire time living out in the woods was leaving out food that might attract animals. If a bear ran its claws along the cabin wall, it wasn't going to be because of something stupid like that. "I'm going to circle the cabin, see what else I can find. You wait here."

"What if you need help?"

"If you hear me scream, come rescue me. Otherwise, wait here. I'm just going to do a quick circle; I'm not going to wander off into the forest."

Rusty stepped off the porch and walked across their front yard. He stayed about ten feet from the cabin so that if there was a nasty surprise waiting around the corner, he wouldn't be face-to-face with it before he saw what he was dealing with.

There might have been footprints. If so, they were filled with water and impossible to identify as such. But there was another very distinct scrape across the wall.

He went around to the back. Another long scrape— this one went from edge to edge—and more imprints in the mud that may or may not have been footprints. There was no question that an animal had done this, and, yes, he was leaning very strongly in a "bear" direction.

No scrapes on the final side of the house. Rusty returned to the front porch.

"Yeah, it scraped up the side and back wall," he told Mia. "I don't think it was actually trying to get inside. If it was, it would dig at the wall, not just run its claws along it."

"So, what, you think it was just committing vandalism?"

"I don't know what it was doing. I don't see any reason to panic, though. It didn't get in and it might not even come back. Most likely, it came by looking for food, didn't find any, and left. We're fine. I mean, we won't be idiots, we'll stick close to the cabin for a day or two, but we're not in any danger."

"I wish we'd made more of an effort to get the truck

free," said Mia.

"We're not going to need to flee our home. The cabin is safe. All that thing did was scrape up the wood a little. If it wanted to get in, it would've already tried."

Rusty believed what he was saying. They'd made the right call on the truck—trying to get it back on the path in those conditions would've been a waste of time. And he wasn't thinking, "Oh, Lord, why oh why have I refused to get a telephone?" They didn't need to call for help. They didn't need to drive into town. Yes, the recent weirdness was disconcerting, but they could handle an aggressive bear-or-whatever without calling for help. Rusty was a good shot, and he had enough ammunition to miss a *lot* of times without running out.

"If we had the truck, we could go into town and get a few bear traps."

"We don't need bear traps. If it gets close enough, we shoot it. If it doesn't get close enough, it doesn't need to die."

"All right," said Mia. "Then what's the next step?"

"It's almost one o'clock. Go back to bed. I'm going to sleep out here so I can be ready to check if I hear something."

"I'm sleeping out here, too."

"I already called the couch."

"Then I'll sleep in a chair."

"Just sleep in your bed with the door open. I promise I'll wake you up if something happens."

"Are you scared?" Mia asked.

"No."

"Are you sure?"

"I'm feeling the need for caution. I'm not frightened."

"Well, I'm scared."

"That's okay," said Rusty. "No shame in it. You're probably just smarter than I am."

"We should have kept trying to find somebody who could tell us what was going on."

"We can spend all night second-guessing our decisions, or we can get some sleep. Personally, I'd rather be well-rested in case we need to run for the truck."

"That wasn't funny."

"It wasn't supposed to be."

"It wasn't reassuring, either."

"It wasn't supposed to be that, either."

"What was it supposed to be?"

"I'm not sure," Rusty admitted. "All I'm saying is, maybe we screwed up, maybe we didn't. We can't change it, so why make things more difficult for ourselves? Let's get some rest. Even if we forget about the bear or whatever, we've still got an hour-long walk, so why be exhausted when we do it?"

"I don't think I'll be able to fall asleep. You go to bed and I'll keep watch."

Rusty started to protest, but decided there was no reason to *not* let her keep watch. In an absolute worst case scenario, where the creature came back and aggressively tried to get into the cabin, it wasn't as if it could break right through the wall like the Kool-Aid Man. He'd have plenty of time to spring to action. "That sounds fine," he said. "Wake me up if you change your mind."

He went back into his bedroom, leaving the door open, and set the pistol and flashlight on his dresser. He climbed into bed, unsure whether he'd be able to fall asleep himself, but he drifted off moments after he closed his eyes.

"Uncle Rusty?"

Mia was shaking his shoulder. Rusty flinched, forgetting where he was for a moment, and then he remembered and sat up. "What's wrong?"

"I heard a growl."

Rusty got out of bed. They both went into the living room and peered out the window.

"Oh, shit, do you see that?" asked Mia, pointing.

Rusty did. It was too far away from the outside lights of the cabin to be seen clearly, but the silhouette did indeed appear to be a bear. A really freaking big one. Huge.

He went over to get the flashlight then returned to the window. He turned it on and shone the beam through the glass. Too much glare. He couldn't see anything.

The silhouette was slowly moving.

"It's not going to charge at me," said Rusty, mostly believing that as he walked over to the front door.

"How do you know that?" asked Mia. "You didn't think the squirrel was going to leap at you from the tree, either."

"Okay, let me revise that. I'm not going to leave the porch. If it does charge at me, I'll run back inside and slam the door."

"I don't think that's a good idea."

"It's not a supersonic bear. I'll only be a few steps from the door. We need to know what's out there."

Rusty didn't want to keep arguing until the bear left, so he opened the door and stepped outside. He shone the flashlight beam on the animal and, yes, it was a bear. A gigantic grizzly. Biggest one he'd ever seen. Maybe a hundred feet away.

It turned to face him. Rusty couldn't see its eyes clearly, so he didn't know if they were bloodshot, but it sure as hell didn't look like a friendly bear.

The bear began to lumber toward him.

Rusty quickly stepped back into the cabin. He extended his free hand toward Mia. "Give me a gun."

The bear continued moving toward the cabin. It seemed to be in no hurry, but there was no question about its intended destination.

"Get the hell out of here!" Rusty shouted at it. "Go away! You don't belong here! Fuck off!"

The bear did not stop moving. Its eyes glowed in the flashlight beam.

Mia handed Rusty the pistol. He gave her the flashlight. He took aim, not at the bear but directly over it. It was dark and his hands were trembling and you didn't want to shoot a bear unless you knew you were going to get a direct hit.

He squeezed the trigger.

The bear stopped moving. It looked up, as if it had felt the bullet sail over its head.

Then it turned to the side and began to lumber away.

Rusty's mouth fell open and he dropped the gun. He couldn't be seeing this right.

Mia kept the flashlight beam pointed at the bear's side. They could see its ribs.

Not in a "the bear was starving and emaciated" manner.

Though the bear looked otherwise healthy and alert, they could see its exposed ribcage.

JEFF STRAND

CHAPTER SEVEN

R usty slammed the door.

There would be no more sleep tonight.

He didn't need to ask Mia if she'd seen that. Her hand was clamped over her mouth and she looked positively horrified.

Now he regretted not owning a telephone and leaving the truck stuck in the mud.

If not for his encounter with the squirrel, Rusty could come up with a logical explanation for the bear's condition. It could have a flesh-eating bacteria, or been seriously injured in a fight with a wolf or another bear. An exposed ribcage didn't necessarily mean that it couldn't walk around like a normal bear, right? It wasn't as if its guts were trailing behind it. Everything seemed to still be contained.

Yet after what the squirrel had done, there was no way to simply say, "Yep, this is a quaint but natural occurrence." Rusty wasn't ready to commit to the idea of a zombie bear yet. It might not be, or have been, dead. But there was *something* wrong with this bear that went beyond "afflicted with a flesh-eating bacteria," and if Mia went with zombie bear, he wasn't going to correct her.

Mia removed her hand from her mouth. "You saw that, right?"

"Yes."

"I mean the ribs."

"Yes. I saw it."

Mia didn't ask what he thought was wrong with it. She must've known that he had no answer. She hurried over to the front window and looked out. "It's coming back."

Rusty rushed over and looked for himself, even though there was no reason to doubt his niece. "Okay," he said. "No big deal. No big deal. We've got bigger guns."

He took the shotgun out of the cabinet. Then he peeked through the window again, hoping the bear had changed its mind. It hadn't.

He was pretty sure the bear couldn't get inside the cabin, at least not without significant effort, but better to blow it away than to let it cause serious damage to his home. And then he'd kidnap Dr. Teal, bring him out here, and force him to conduct a scientific investigation at gunpoint.

Rusty opened the front door. Thank God the bear was still moving slowly. It was about fifty feet away. If it had a sudden surge of velocity, Rusty could still get back inside in time.

"I told you to get the fuck out of here!" he shouted at it, as he took careful aim with the shotgun. Then he raised his aim a bit. The shotgun would make a much louder bang than the pistol, and that might be sufficient to frighten it away for good. If he fired directly at it and didn't kill it, he could have an enraged bear coming at him.

He squeezed the trigger.

The bear flinched as if he'd startled it. It stopped walking but didn't turn away.

"The next one goes in your face," he shouted, hoping the bear would understand his intent if not his words.

The bear resumed walking toward him.

"Shit," said Rusty. He lowered his aim. He took a moment to concentrate on making his arm stop trembling, put the bear's head in his sight, and then squeezed the trigger.

Too low. He hit the creature, but in its chest, or whatever that part was called on a bear. Its fur burst open without blood. The bear let out a roar of pain.

It stopped moving again, but didn't run away.

Rusty was pretty sure he now had an enraged bear in front of him.

The bear looked at him. Its bloodshot eyes were clearly visible. A large flap of brown fur dangled where it had been shot. When it snarled at him, Rusty didn't know if it was *consciously* showing off its many sharp teeth, but he got the message.

"You only get one more chance!" he informed the bear, hoping it was in a lot of pain and receptive to being scared away by threats.

It continued to stare at him. And then walked toward him.

Rusty might have had enough time to reload the shotgun before it reached the front porch. Or he might not. The consequences of being a little too slow or dropping a shell with his trembling hands were really freaking dire, so he decided that this was not the best time to test out his speed. He went back into the cabin, then slammed and locked the door.

"It's still coming," said Mia, looking out the window. She held her rifle against her chest.

"It can't get inside," said Rusty, who, as of a minute ago, no longer believed that.

"It's on the porch."

"Get away from the window."

Mia did. Rusty popped open the shotgun, removed the empty shells, then accidentally dropped the two replacement ones onto the floor, so it was probably for the best that he hadn't decided to face off against the bear. He scooped them up and reloaded the shotgun.

There was a loud thump and the door shook on its hinges as the bear struck it. Though Rusty couldn't see what was happening out there, it sounded more like the bear had bashed the wood with its paws than trying to smash through it at a run. That was good. The door could keep out a bear that attempted to pound it down— probably—but it wasn't going to withstand an animal that size coming at it like a battering ram.

Of course, the front window was problematic.

Another thump. The door held.

Rusty and Mia kept a safe distance—not that there was a safe distance inside the cabin if a goddamn undead grizzly bear got in there—and pointed their respective guns at the door.

Another thump and the top right corner of the door jutted forward.

It was definitely pounding on the wood with its paws, and Rusty's belief that the door would keep it out was clearly wrong. Two or three more slams and that door was coming completely off its hinges, no question.

Rusty was wrong about that, too. It only took one

more slam.

The front door toppled forward, shaking the entire cabin as it struck the floor. A couple of the floorboards broke on impact. Mia screamed but didn't panic. She kept her rifle focused on the now-open doorway. If they lived through this, Rusty would tell her how proud he was of the way she'd handled this situation.

The bear let out a loud snort and stuck its head through the doorway.

"Don't shoot yet," Rusty said.

The grizzly bear's massive size was not a good thing, overall, but it did give Rusty and Mia one advantage at the moment: the animal was too big to fit through the doorway.

Oh, there was no question that it could widen the doorway if it really wanted to. Rusty's hope, possibly delusional, was that the bear would get frustrated and give up if it had to work to get at them.

The bear let out an angry roar. Mia screamed again, and Rusty somehow kept from wetting his pajama bottoms.

They weren't trapped in here, technically. There was a large window behind them in the kitchen and a smaller one in each of their bedrooms, so worst-case scenario, they could escape that way. But Rusty was far more confident in his ability to keep the bear out of the cabin than to outrun it. Fleeing their home would be a last resort.

The bear roared again. The sound was terrifying, but the beast could roar all it wanted as long as it didn't try to get inside.

Then it stepped forward, squeezing itself into the doorway. It obviously wasn't going to fit all the way through that opening, so the question was how long the frame would last. Since Rusty could already hear the wood cracking, the answer seemed to be: not long.

More cracking, and a large chunk of wood fell to the floor.

"I think we should shoot it now," said Mia.

Rusty nodded and squeezed the trigger. The shotgun blast got the bear right in the face, blowing off most of its lower jaw. Teeth scattered everywhere. Its tongue, half-gone, dangled from what remained of its mouth, not bleeding.

Mia fired her rifle, sending a bullet directly into the hole that already existed in its chest.

Rusty fired again. This shot wasn't as impactful as the first, blowing off most of the bear's left ear.

Mia fired three shots in a row. The first hit the bear in the chest again, but lower, creating a new hole. The second missed, putting a hole in the wall inches from the doorway. The third struck the bear in the side of the face.

This time when the bear roared, it was with pain instead of fury. It backed out of the doorway and disappeared from sight.

Rusty quickly reloaded.

Mia walked across the living room to get a better view from the window. "It's still on the porch," she said. A moment later, her report became unnecessary as the bear walked right in front of the glass.

"Should we open fire?" Rusty asked. "Just pump as many bullets into it as we can?"

"If the bear's fucked up, and the squirrel was fucked up, lots of other animals could be fucked up, too. What if we have to run for the truck and fend them off? We should conserve our ammo."

She was right. They had a generous supply of ammunition from the perspective of hunting and target practice. When you added "defending themselves during a three mile run through a forest full of nightmare creatures" the ammunition situation didn't seem quite as optimistic.

That said, they had no idea how widespread this was. There was the squirrel, the bear, and whatever had killed the deer, which could've been the bear. That might be as far as it went. Still, Rusty agreed with Mia that they shouldn't go all Bonnie and Clyde on the bear unless it became absolutely necessary.

The bear walked past the window.

Mia moved again to get a different angle. "It's still there," she said. "It sat down."

"Maybe it's dying."

"It doesn't look like it's dying. It looks like it's waiting."

How long would a bear wait for prey after the lower half of its jaw had been blown off? Surely at some point it would slink off to tend to its wounds. A normal bear would be bleeding out by now.

Rusty and Mia could outwait the bear. They could outwait it even if it decided to settle in for a few days; they had plenty of food. Though it would be nice if they also had a front door.

They had the tools necessary to nail the door back in place...but those were in the shed. They'd either have to stroll onto the front porch past the bear or sneak out a bedroom window. The door hadn't done any good before and a newly nailed one wouldn't withstand a second attack, but if other animals less powerful than a bear were affected, they'd be glad to have a front door to keep them out.

Rusty didn't want to take the risk quite yet. They'd keep tabs on the bear through the window, watch the doorway closely, and see how this played out.

Mia wiped a tear from her eye. Rusty wouldn't have blamed her if she succumbed to hysterical shrieking and mad cackling laughter, so a tear was amazingly brave. He felt like he was one more bear-roar from weeping himself.

"Changed my mind," he said.

"What?" Mia asked. Rusty realized that he hadn't said anything about his shed plan out loud. He was losing it a bit. They couldn't afford for him to do that if they were going to survive this.

"We've got a hammer and nails in the shed. To nail the door back up in case something smaller tries to get in. I was thinking that we should wait until the bear left, but right now we know exactly where it is. If you keep an eye on it, I can go out a window and get the stuff. You just shout out to me if the bear moves."

"Are you sure we don't have anything already in the cabin?" Mia asked.

"Not that I can think of."

"Couldn't we just prop the door up and push some furniture against it?"

Rusty thought about that. "Yes," he said. "That's a much better idea."

He set the shotgun on the floor. As he crouched next to the fallen door, Mia moved to help him. He waved her away. "Stay on bear watch. I'll ask for help if I need it."

Mia nodded and returned to her best view of the bear through the window. Rusty placed his hands underneath the top of the door and lifted it. He didn't remember it being this heavy when he installed it in the first place, but he'd been twenty-five years younger back then.

It had really damaged the floor. Not to the point of breaking all the way through, but he had some serious repair work to do when this was over. It felt good to know that he could think about something like this, rather than the idea of fleeing the cabin and never, ever coming back.

He pushed the door against the frame. Though it left a little more of a gap than he wanted, he was worried that if he centered it any more it might drop right through. "Bear still sitting?" he asked.

"Still sitting."

He shoved the couch across the floor and in front of the door. It successfully kept the door upright. It wouldn't keep out hordes of invaders, but it was far better than nothing.

"It's getting up," said Mia.

Rusty picked up the shotgun. It took him a moment to remember if he'd loaded it or not. Yeah, he had.

He no longer needed Mia to report on the bear's status, because it walked in front of the window again. It let out a snort, though he couldn't hear it, then pressed its mangled face against the glass.

"Doesn't that *hurt*?" Mia wondered aloud. If Rusty had just had his lower jaw shot off, he wouldn't be pressing his face against anything. He couldn't deny that he felt kind of sorry for the poor animal. It quite clearly felt pain, but its brain was so messed up that it didn't care.

It licked the glass with what remained of its tongue.

The bear was free to lick the glass and do whatever other creepy stuff it wanted, as long as it didn't try to get inside. Eventually it would have to leave, to find a more convenient meal or to shit in the woods.

It moved its head away from the window.

Let out another roar—back to rage instead of pain.

Then it smashed one of its paws against the window, shattering the glass.

CHAPTER EIGHT

Shards of glass rained down upon the floor. The bear lunged with its other paw, breaking even more of the glass. It leaned halfway through the window, apparently not caring about the jagged glass on the bottom of the frame that was digging into its underside.

Mia screamed. Rusty screamed.

Then they opened fire.

Rusty's first shot removed the top of the bear's head, and the fact that it continued to climb through the window after this was evidence that the world had changed in a big bad way. Mia fired a couple of shots into it. It wasn't correct to say that they had no impact; the bear clearly felt them, they just weren't enough to kill it, severely injure it, or dissuade it from continuing to climb into the cabin.

If it was still coming after them with part of its brain exposed, it was going to take a lot more than shooting it a few more times to make it stop. The squirrel had eventually quit moving, but it was in terrible shape before that happened. Doing that much damage to a fully mature grizzly bear was going to be quite a bit more difficult.

Maybe a direct blast to the face with a shotgun would be enough.

Rusty squeezed the trigger.

It should've been an easy shot, considering that the bear was right there in his living room, but the bear dropped to the floor just as he fired. The shotgun cut a thick swath across the fur on its back.

Mia fired two more shots. Both completely missed. Rusty suspected that she'd been aiming for its eyes. He had a lot of experience with guns and *he* couldn't hit a bear in the eyes, even at close quarters.

Without either of them shouting, "Let's run for the bedroom!" they simultaneously decided that it was the right thing to do. Rusty scooped up the box of shotgun shells and they ran into Mia's bedroom. She slammed the door.

The rifle ammo was still in the living room, but Mia should have a few shots left, and they weren't doing any good anyway. For right now they were in "flight" mode.

Rusty could hear the bear moving around, knocking stuff over. An angry grizzly could really do some serious damage to their cabin, which was more than a little upsetting, but he'd worry about their property after they escaped with their lives.

He reloaded the shotgun while Mia opened her window. They didn't have to worry that the bear might have snuck outside and was heading back there; the damn thing was making so much noise in their home that they'd have no problem at all keeping tabs on it. He was a little surprised that it wasn't trying to break down the bedroom door—it had seen them go in there—but he *had* blown off the top of its head, which was the kind of thing that impacted decision making.

"Do you need me to help you get out?" Mia asked. Rusty couldn't really be offended by the offer. Climbing out of windows, even first-story ones, wasn't something he'd done since he was a teenager.

"I will, yeah," he said. "But maybe I should try to get in a couple more shots, first."

"No. That's a shitty idea."

"It's not like bullets are bouncing off of it. If I can get in a couple of good head shots, we might have a lot less of a threat to deal with."

"What if you open that door and it mauls you?"

"We can hear it! It's destroying the kitchen! We open the door, squeeze off a shot or two, then go out the window."

"I don't agree with this plan," said Mia. "I'm not going to try to stop you, but I don't agree with it. I think we should just go."

Rusty was willing to admit that his niece might be absolutely correct. But his plan seemed low risk and potentially high return. He wasn't going to walk up and smack the bear on the snout; he was going to shoot it from the "safety" of the bedroom. Then they'd immediately revert to the plan of getting the hell out of the cabin. If the bear ripped off one of his arms, Mia would be welcome to say, "I told you so."

"I hear you," he said. "All I need is ten seconds."

He stood by the door and listened. He didn't need to listen *carefully* because he could hear metal pots and pans hitting the floor. Unless the bear could teleport—something that, admittedly, seemed less impossible than it might have yesterday—he was at higher risk of shooting himself in the foot than being disemboweled by the bear.

He opened the bedroom door just a crack, held up the shotgun, then kicked the door open all the way.

An entire mounted cabinet came crashing onto the kitchen counter. The cabinet door fell open and broken dishes spilled out onto the floor and into the sink. This pissed Rusty off enough that he stopped feeling sorry for the bear's facial injuries. It was up on its hind legs, and its head brushed against the ceiling.

It dropped to all fours and turned around to face him.

Rusty took careful but quick aim, then fired.

He got it in the shoulder, sending up a spray of fur and meat but not blowing off another chunk of its head like he'd intended.

The bear ran at him.

Rusty fired again. This time he was too scared to aim properly, and he knew before he even saw the impact that his shot had been worthless. It blasted a hole in the fallen cabinet, shattering some more dishes.

He slammed and locked the bedroom door.

Okay, he'd hoped to do quite a bit more damage to the bear, but at least he hadn't been mauled. For right now, he was happy with any action that wasn't a disastrous blunder.

Mia seemed to have waited just long enough to be sure that his severed head didn't bounce across the floor. She leapt out the window, then leaned back in to assist him. He handed her the shotgun and the box of ammunition. Earlier, twenty shells had seemed like plenty. Now it seemed woefully insufficient.

The bedroom door burst open.

Once again, the bear was bigger than the frame. So

they weren't in immediate danger. But this could turn into immediate danger pretty quickly, and Rusty wasn't convinced that the bear couldn't squeeze through the doorway if it was persistent. He definitely needed to stick with the plan of getting the hell out of the cabin.

With minor assistance from Mia, he climbed out the window. As he looked back, the bear swiped at him with a paw that was about twelve feet away.

"Should we hide in the shed?" Mia asked.

The shed was much more vulnerable in the instance of an angry bear attack than the cabin, but it was safer than trying to get to the truck. If nothing else, it would give them a few moments to catch their breath and try to work out a plan.

"Yeah," said Rusty.

They ran into the shed. The door didn't lock from the inside, but if the bear wanted to get in, a lock wasn't going to do any good anyway. The shed was full of completed furniture, works in progress, lumber, and tools. A spare vehicle, a motorcycle maybe, would've been nice, but he'd never needed one. If they survived this, he'd get one for sure.

"I think we can still kill it," said Mia. "We just need to get in a position where we can keep shooting at it without it being able to get us. If we hit it enough times there eventually won't be enough of its head left for it to find us. Maybe we should climb a tree."

"Bears can climb trees."

"But would it keep coming after us if we were shooting it? It wouldn't keep climbing if you kept blasting it with the shotgun. You might even blow off one of its legs. A three-legged bear can't climb a tree."

"What if it *does* keep coming after us? We'd be

trapped."

"What's your better plan?" asked Mia.

"I don't have a better plan. I just don't like that one." He glanced around the shed. "What about the chainsaw?"

"What *about* the chainsaw?"

"We could make a three-legged bear with it."

"Yeah, if you wanna walk right up to it! Fighting it off with a chainsaw is what you do when every other plan has failed."

"Well, it can't hurt to keep it with us." Rusty walked over and picked up the chainsaw. He supposed that it could indeed hurt to keep it with them, since carrying both the shotgun and the chainsaw would make it awkward to run. Still, he could always just drop it if they needed to make a hasty retreat.

"There's also the axe out by the firewood," said Mia.

"Yes! Axe, chainsaw, shotgun, rifle...that's more than enough to defend ourselves against that thing. We're in good shape." He wished that he was paranoid instead of just deeply antisocial. Then he'd have explosives and an underground bunker.

"What now? Do we just hide in here?"

That had been Rusty's original idea, but now he was questioning that decision. If it was a normal bear, sure, he'd feel confident that it wouldn't find them here, but who knew what a zombie bear or whatever this thing was would do? It couldn't easily get out of the cabin except to go back through the window, so perhaps he should take advantage of it being in a relatively confined space. He wouldn't go back inside the cabin, of course, but if he shot at it through the windows he might actually be able to blow its head or a leg off. Granted, this meant that the bear would not be able to find its own way out of his home; still, that was a problem that could be solved later.

Though he wasn't fond of the idea of blowing holes into his beloved cabin, it was certainly less damage than what the bear was doing right now. He didn't think that the bear, left alone, could bring the whole structure to the ground, but it could easily make the place uninhabitable. He had neither the funds nor the inclination to bring professionals out here, so he and Mia would be making all of the repairs themselves.

"I'm going back out to shoot it," he said.

"That's—"

"I'm not going inside the cabin. I'm only shooting it from safe spaces."

Mia's progression of thoughts were clearly visible on her face: *That's a horrible idea and I should talk him out of it....Actually, he's going to do it anyway so why waste time talking?...And if he's going to do it anyway, I might as well help.*

"How can I help?"

"Hold the chainsaw."

"Okay." She set down the rifle and picked up the chainsaw. She kept the flashlight in her other hand.

Rusty opened the door, half expecting a horror movie jump scare where the bear was *right there*, jaws wide open, but of course it wasn't, and it didn't have a lower jaw anyway.

He could hear the bear still inside the cabin, breaking more stuff. He waited a few moments, and the sounds of destruction never let up. He didn't know if the bear was confused and scared and flailing around, if it was trying to claw through a wall to escape, or if it was just being an asshole.

They walked over to the bedroom window they'd

climbed out of. Rusty set the box of shells on the ground and then rested the barrel of the shotgun against the bottom frame. If he was lucky, the bear would wander past the doorway and he'd get a perfect shot.

"Do you want me to go see which room it's in?" Mia asked.

"No."

"Good."

They waited for about thirty seconds. About two of those seconds were quiet.

"Maybe we should call out to it," said Mia.

"I want to catch it by surprise."

"You'll lose the element of surprise after the first shot. If it hears us and looks into the room, there's more of a chance that you can get it right in the face."

"You're very smart," Rusty told her. "Hey, bear! We're over here! Come and get us!"

Mia joined in. The sound of things breaking stopped and was replaced by the sound of loud bear footsteps.

The bear stepped into view. There were some shards of broken dishes on its back. It turned toward the doorway, looked at them, and let out as much of a roar as it could manage with its mangled face. The sound was pathetic yet terrifying.

Rusty had a clear shot at its head, but he also had a clear shot at its two front legs. Should he try to blow away more of its skull, which might finish it off, or should he try to incapacitate it with a leg wound?

He decided to go for the leg.

He took careful aim, trying to unleash his inner cyborg and hit the target with robotic precision. The shotgun wouldn't blow its leg completely off but if he hit accurately enough he could render the leg useless. He squeezed the trigger.

Much of the bear's front leg blew apart. It let out a...*scream* wasn't the right word, but that's sure as hell what it sounded like. It lost its balance and fell, doing further damage to the floorboards.

The bear had landed perfectly for Rusty to take a shot at its other leg. He fired again. Its other leg tore open, right at the joint. The bear's agonized sounds made it impossible to enjoy any sense of victory, and after he put it out of its misery they'd still have a dead bear in the living room to contend with, but at least the immediate threat was over.

"Uncle Rusty...?"

Mia was not looking at the bear in the living room. Rusty spun around and saw that she was looking at the *other* bear running toward them.

JEFF STRAND

CHAPTER NINE

Mia scrambled back through the open window, taking the chainsaw with her, then immediately turned around and helped pull Rusty inside. He slammed the window shut. A moment later, the new bear, up on its hind legs, was right there. It wasn't as if Rusty had escaped being disemboweled by mere inches, but this was *way* too close.

He scooted away from the glass, chest tightening, unable to breathe, feeling like he was on the verge of an all-out panic attack. The bear moved out of sight. Rusty didn't know if it had left or merely dropped to all fours. Though it wasn't as big as the other grizzly inside of their cabin, it was still a fully-grown bear.

Mia, to her credit, could at least breathe well enough to talk. "Oh my God..."

Rusty wanted to reassure her that they were going to be fine, but he'd have to wait until he was no longer suffocating. He might even be having a heart attack.

He glanced back. The bear in the doorway was trying to bite at them, even though all it could do was lunge with its upper jaw. How could an animal in this condition still care about getting at its prey? It was in no condition to continue its rampage inside the cabin, but Rusty sure as hell wouldn't try to get past the thing without putting a few more bullets into it.

At the sound of something scraping against glass, he returned his attention to the window. Not surprisingly, it was the bear's claws. The bear was looking right at him with its bloodshot eyes, leaving thick trails down the window. If it weren't a bear, Rusty would've thought that the creature was making a conscious effort to be frightening, like Freddy Krueger scraping his finger knives along metal.

Rusty forced himself to calm down and take a breath. Yes, this was a remarkably shitty situation, but the new bear probably couldn't get into the cabin, and the old bear couldn't get into the bedroom. And he still had...

He cursed.

"What's wrong?" Mia asked, because it was clear from his tone that something was wrong beyond the obvious problem of them being trapped between two bears.

"The shotgun shells are outside."

It took Mia a moment to respond. "Oh."

This was pretty bad. One thing Rusty most definitely did not want to do was fight these things up close. He supposed he could be forgiven for accidentally leaving behind the ammunition when there was a bear charging at him, but still, this was going to make matters significantly more difficult.

He wished the injured bear would go silent. He didn't want to pity it.

The outside bear placed its paws against the top of the window, and then again slowly dragged its claws down the glass, creating a new set of deep scratches along with small cracks along the way. The glass held, but Rusty didn't think it would if the bear did this a third time. It was the *slowness* of its action that gave him the feeling, preposterous as it was, that the bear was doing this on purpose to be scary. And it was succeeding.

The bear put back its head and roared at them, showing off lots and lots of teeth. Then it stared at Rusty as if daring him not to look away in terror.

We're safe, he tried to tell himself, even though he wasn't convinced that the bear couldn't simply start prying the boards off the cabin wall. *We're safe. We're fine. It's all cool.*

The bear scratched a third set of claw marks down the glass. The window miraculously held, though it was harder to see through now.

Okay, they couldn't just stand here cowering. They had to go on the offensive.

Rusty set down the shotgun and picked up the chainsaw.

"What the hell are you going to do?" Mia asked.

Rusty's arm plus the chainsaw was not longer than the bear's reach, so he'd be putting himself at risk for joining the first bear in the "missing half your face" club. But a whirring chainsaw blade across the snout might dissuade the bear from entering the cabin, or he might even be able to lop off its front paws.

"What do you think I'm gonna do?" he asked.

He tugged the starting cord. Truthfully, if the chainsaw had failed to start after a couple of tries he probably would've lost his courage, but it roared to life on the first attempt.

The bear, apparently not intimidated, scraped its claws

yet again. A large triangle-shaped piece of glass fell out and shattered against the floor. More glass followed. It wasn't as if the bear couldn't simply have broken the window any time it wanted, but still, this left Rusty feeling extremely exposed. A guy holding a chainsaw should feel way more powerful than this.

He and Mia backed away as the bear leaned through the window, breaking out most of what remained of the glass. It was too big to squeeze through. At least that's what Rusty kept telling himself. Like the first one, this bear seemed unconcerned about the broken glass on the bottom of the window frame.

The bear continued to climb in. The bedroom window was quite a bit smaller than the living room window, and it was simply not possible that a fully-grown grizzly bear could get through it. Not a chance. Hell, if they were lucky, the bear would get stuck and be completely helpless.

With its head and front legs inside the window...the bear did indeed seem to be stuck!

But Rusty could hear the wood cracking.

The other bear had somehow scooted closer to the bedroom doorway. Not only was it biting at them with its half-face, but it was clawing at them with its mangled front legs. Though the bear was in ghastly shape, it had their exit blocked.

The outdoor bear apparently wasn't *stuck* stuck, and it leaned most of the way back out of the window. It placed its paws against the window frame. Then it tore out a large chunk of the wood.

No reason to freak out yet. The window frame would naturally be less sturdy than the rest of the wall. Oh, this was certainly bad—very, very bad—but they didn't need to go absolutely batshit with terror quite yet.

Time to make the bear reconsider trying to rip the wall apart.

Rusty wanted to explain to Mia what he was about to do, but she wouldn't be able to hear him over the chainsaw anyway. So he just strode forward, holding the chainsaw in front of him with both hands, and lunged at the bear.

He got it right in the snout, making its nose disintegrate before the bear pulled completely out of the window.

But it didn't leave.

How the hell did that thing take a chainsaw to the snout and not leave? What was wrong with it? Zombie bear or not, why wouldn't it flee back into the woods after that? It took a *whirring chainsaw blade right in its face*! You ran away after that shit! It was the way of nature! What could possibly have happened in this forest to make the inhabitants not care if their nose got sawed off?

The bear stood back up and placed its paws against the opening again. Then it tore off the rest of the bottom of the window frame.

The opening was still too narrow for the bear to squeeze through, but if it ripped off a couple of planks, that might no longer be the case. If they didn't do something, they'd have to assume that there'd be a murderous bear in the bedroom very soon.

Mia tapped the wall and mimed using the chainsaw.

Yes, they could in theory saw a hole in the wall and pass from Mia's bedroom to Rusty's. But their bedroom doors weren't all that far apart, and if the bear in the living room turned itself around it might end up being just as much of a threat there as it was here. Rusty also wasn't convinced that he could saw his way through the wall before the outside bear widened the window opening enough to join them indoors.

To get out of this, he was going to have to use the chainsaw on a bear instead of the wall. And, of course, when choosing between the two bears, it made sense to go after the one that should by any reasonable standard already be dead.

Its front legs were in hideous shape and it was missing a front jaw. How badly could it hurt him even if it did get in a swipe?

He took a step toward it. Then he glanced over at Mia to see if she was giving him a "What the hell do you think you're doing?" look. Surprisingly, she wasn't. In fact, she'd picked up the shotgun and was holding it by the barrel, as if prepared to use it as a bludgeoning weapon.

He returned his attention to the bear. He didn't want to do this. He really, really didn't want to do this. There was no part of him that wanted to take a chainsaw to a grizzly bear. But he didn't really have a choice, and in fact knew that he should be acting now instead of thinking about how much he didn't want to do this.

He allowed himself to close his eyes for exactly two seconds to work up his nerve, then walked over to the bear, crouched down, and pressed the chainsaw blade against its left leg at the joint. It wasn't hanging on by much after the shotgun blast, and it came loose pretty easily. He pressed the chainsaw against its right leg, which was in better shape but also did not resist the whirring blade. Bits of fur and flesh (but again, no blood) flew up into his face.

Rusty was glad that the chainsaw was too loud for him

to hear the bear's reaction. But it violently thrashed around and tried to bite him.

Mia, doing her part, smacked the bear's front legs out of the way with the handle of the shotgun.

Rusty wanted to neatly saw off its head, but the angle wasn't right to get at its neck. Even missing most of its front legs, he felt like the bear could harm him, so he brought the chainsaw blade down against the center of its head, pressing it into its already exposed brain. The bear twitched like it had been hit with a massive jolt of electricity. Rusty kept pushing until the chainsaw hit the floor underneath.

The bear lifted its head. The two halves flopped to separate sides.

He wanted to take a moment to just gape at this, but there was no time.

He did glance back at the other bear, which was in the process of ripping down another plank from the cabin wall. Shit. Couldn't worry about that now. He returned his attention to the bear with the bisected head. It was still moving, flicking scraps of brain matter around. Rusty could hear Mia screaming over the sound of the chainsaw.

At this point, while the thrashing bear posed a threat to Rusty's mental health, it didn't seem to be a physical threat anymore, so he got even closer and slammed the blade against its neck. It was moving around too much for it to be a clean cut, but he got a jagged diagonal slice and the bear's head came off.

Though the bear's head stopped moving—apart from the rolling motion when it hit the floor—the rest of the bear did not.

Sure, this could be similar to the "like a chicken with

its head cut off" thing or the way a fish would keep flopping around after its decapitation. But a bear was supposed to cease all movement after its head was removed with a chainsaw. All goddamn movement!

That said, the bear's headless body seemed quite a bit less threatening than the whole bear had been, and Rusty felt much more comfortable with the idea of getting close to it and going absolutely freaking nuts with the chainsaw.

He pressed the blade into the bear's back and began to saw.

It wasn't a tidy dismemberment. The bear was far too large to simply slice it down the middle, so Rusty had to saw off large chunks. After several pieces of the bear were missing, he felt safe enough to squeeze past it so that he could get at its back legs. He cut those off as close to the torso as he could. And with that, the only danger the bear posed was if it rolled over on somebody, and it wasn't rolling very much anymore.

Rusty glanced back at Mia. He expected her to look shocked and horrified by the carnage, and got exactly what he expected.

A more noteworthy sight was that the other bear was trying to climb through the window frame, which now seemed almost large enough to accommodate it. If it had taken the time to rip off one more plank, it would've fit easily, but instead it was squeezing through, and there was little reason to believe that it wouldn't succeed.

Rusty didn't want to fight this bear right now, but he knew that "bear stuck in window frame" was a better opponent than "bear roaming around bedroom." Before he could change his mind, he rushed toward it, chainsaw roaring.

The bear took a swipe at him. It struck the chainsaw blade, lopping off the top half of its paw even though that hadn't been Rusty's intent. One of its severed digits hit Rusty in the mouth. When the bear let out a roar, Rusty could feel its hot breath on his face; stuck or not, chainsaw or not, this was *terrifying*. He almost wanted to flee and save the bear for another time.

But no. This was his best chance.

He went for the rest of its thrashing leg, sawing off the entire paw. It swiped at him with its other paw and almost got him. Rusty thrust the chainsaw blade at it, trying to aim higher so as to sever a larger portion of its leg, and got it in the joint. Half of its leg dropped to the floor.

The bear lashed out frantically with what remained of its legs.

It seemed to pose no danger now. It couldn't climb the rest of the way inside with only stumps for front legs, and if it managed to pull itself back outside it wouldn't be any danger unless he walked right up to it. Still, he felt like he should finish it off.

He pressed the blade against its neck and pushed down. About halfway through the process, the chainsaw sputtered, then died.

Rusty grabbed the chainsaw cord.

"Don't," said Mia.

Rusty turned back to look at her. "Why not?"

"This is our proof. Nobody can say we're lying if we've still got the living dead bear right here."

Rusty nodded. "You're right. You should've said something before I started sawing off its head."

"I did. You couldn't hear me."

"You should've tapped me on the shoulder."

"While you were holding a running chainsaw?"

"Good point." Rusty tugged on the chainsaw. It was firmly imbedded in the bear's neck and didn't pop free. "Damn it."

"Do you need help?"

"No, I've got it." Rusty tugged a few more times. "Wow, it's really stuck in there."

The bear let out a roar and made a worthless attempt to attack him.

"Maybe it's cruel not to just put it out of its misery," said Mia. "It's probably in a lot of pain."

"What about our proof?"

"All of a sudden I don't think that proof is worth letting the poor thing suffer."

Rusty stared at the bear for a moment. It did seem to be in a lot of pain, although he would not have referred to it as "the poor thing." It was a homicidal asshole of a bear and deserved its fate.

He pulled the starter cord and the chainsaw roared back to life. He resumed the process of sawing off the bear's head, until the chainsaw sputtered and died again.

Its head lolled forward, but not enough that it would fall off on its own. If they each grabbed a side, Rusty figured that he and Mia could tear it off with some effort, but of course they weren't going to take the risk.

He pulled the cord. Nothing.

Again. Nothing.

"Is it out of gas?" Mia asked.

"Could be." Rusty tried to tug the blade out of the bear's neck. "It's stuck in a bone."

The bear roared. It wasn't as loud of a roar as before, but the chainsaw hadn't reached its vocal cords yet and it still had plenty of volume left.

"The other bear is still moving," said Mia.

"Seriously?"

"Yeah. I mean, not much, but it's still twitching. I can get past it, though. Back in a minute."

Without waiting for them to discuss the matter, Mia leapt over the bear pieces in the doorway and hurried off to wherever she was going.

Rusty continued yanking on the cord. He almost felt like he should offer some words of comfort to the creature. "Sorry," he muttered. "I'd hoped for a cleaner cut, but sometimes shit happens."

The bear roared at him. It was moving back and forth; Rusty couldn't tell if it was trying to get inside the cabin or pull itself back out.

He pulled on the cord a couple more times then decided that he was just wasting energy. Hopefully he wouldn't *need* to conserve energy, but for now he should probably assume that there was much more unpleasantness in store before his next nap.

He noticed that the bear's severed paws were moving on the floor. Though they weren't crawling toward him with hostile intent, it was still an unnerving sight.

There was a clatter from the living room as Mia dropped some stuff onto the floor, and then she leapt over the dismembered bear back into her bedroom. She had their axe.

"Here," she said, handing it to him. "No motor required."

"Thanks."

It wasn't a quick and easy process, especially with the imbedded chainsaw in the way, but finally the bear's head dropped to the floor. Rusty, who felt he'd been admirably brave throughout this ordeal, let out a soft yelp as the head rolled toward his foot.

Mia didn't laugh at him.

Rusty pulled the chainsaw free. The bear was still wedged in the window.

"Fine," he said. "Zombie bears."

CHAPTER TEN

"What do you think could've caused it?" Mia asked.

"Radiation. Contaminated water. Scientific experimentation gone amok. Witchcraft. God. Satan. Lots of possibilities. It doesn't matter. What matters is whether it's a squirrel and two bears or if we've got an entire forest full of undead animals."

"I'm rooting for a squirrel and two bears."

"Me too," said Rusty. "One thing I can say is that we're not walking three miles in the dark without knowing what might be out there. So we need to board these windows up until dawn."

"I already brought in some boards from the shed. We should go right out and get more, and the tools."

Rusty nodded. Mia leapt over the bear with little effort. Rusty was a little more hesitant—not because of his age; he just didn't like the idea of jumping over twitching bear parts. He considered chopping them up some more with the axe first, but he and Mia were kind of in a rush, so he overcame his reluctance, made the leap, and nothing grabbed him. Rusty picked up the flashlight and they climbed out of the front window. He shone the light around and saw nothing unsafe.

The shed was close and they wanted to be able to carry as much as possible, but still, Rusty wasn't willing to put down the axe, even for a few moments and even if it saved them a trip. If he was going to die tonight, he didn't want it to be because he'd been stupid enough to go outside without a weapon.

They made two short trips to the shed, both of which were mercifully uneventful. They brought in two hammers, a large box of nails, a plastic gallon container of gasoline, and plenty of boards. This was far more boards than they'd need to cover the windows, but a lot could happen between now and sunrise. Rusty also retrieved the box of shotgun shells he'd so foolishly left outside.

Rusty and Mia went right to work on the front window. One advantage to their profession was that they were both very good with hammers and nails, and they covered it very quickly, leaving a narrow gap to see through.

Rusty pointed to the bear parts on the floor. "Let's get these out of here before we board up the front door."

He refueled the chainsaw, then began the task of cutting the bear into small enough pieces to move. The chainsaw blade dug into the wood after passing through the bear, but Rusty was past worrying about that sort of thing. There was a crapload of damage to repair, so he might as well mess up a few more floorboards.

When the bear was in sufficiently small chunks, Rusty moved the front door and the couch out of the way. Then he used a broom to move the potentially dangerous pieces—the head and four paws—out the front doorway, onto the porch, and then onto the ground. He handed the broom to Mia so she could continue the process with the smaller pieces while he removed others by (gloved) hand. They were being extremely efficient.

Rusty chuckled.

"What?" Mia asked.

"You're humming while you work."

"No, I'm not."

"Yes, you are." Mia often hummed while she worked. Rusty loved that she kept doing it even when the task was removing the parts of a chainsaw-dismembered bear from their cabin. "Keep at it. It's soothing."

"Well, now I'm self-conscious about it."

"I shouldn't have said anything."

"I'll just switch to something that you'll never get out of your head."

"'It's A Small World After All'?"

"I don't know that song."

Now was not the time to think about Mia's lack of cultural references. "Put your gloves on," Rusty told her. "Time to move the big pieces."

The lack of blood made the task more pleasant than it might have been, but it was still pretty horrifically gross. At least the torso chunks weren't moving around. Rusty and Mia each took a side and, with a few trips, carried the rest of the bear outside and tossed it off the porch.

"Do you think we'd turn into zombies if we ate the meat?" Mia asked.

"Are you asking hypothetically or because you already snuck a piece?"

"Hypothetically."

"I think we'd get sick and die, but I don't think we'd

rise from the dead."

They began to board up the door. It was going to be a bitch to pry these off in the morning, but Rusty wanted the cabin to be as secure as possible throughout the night, even if they slept in shifts. (Or, in Rusty's case, possibly never slept again.)

"Can we make a deal?" Mia asked. "If something happens to either one of us, and they come back, the other person will chop them up, no questions asked?"

"Honestly, if I died and came back, I'd rather you tried to reach the small bit of humanity that was still inside of me."

"I'm being serious."

"So am I."

"These animals are more hostile than regular animals, so it stands to reason that we'd be hostile if we came back. If I'm coming after you, I don't *want* you to try to reason with me. I want you to lop off my head."

"I guess I'd trust you to use your best judgment," said Rusty. "You'd feel bad if you cut off my head and found out later that you just needed to make me think about a fond memory. Anyway, it's irrelevant. We're out of danger."

"We're going to be in a lot more danger tomorrow."

"Not if it was just a squirrel and two bears."

"Do you believe that it was?" Mia asked.

"No." Rusty sighed. "If I had to place a bet on it, I'd say that yeah, we're going to be in some danger when we go after the truck. But we don't know the scope of this. Maybe it's only happening to animals that drank from a certain stream. And maybe they *are* dead, and it's only the ones that died of some other cause after they drank from the stream. We may have already encountered the worst of it."

"It's possible," said Mia, though Rusty could tell that she was leaning much more toward "the entire forest is full of undead horrors."

"Anyway, we'll bring lots of weapons and we'll be extremely careful. I truly believe that we'll be fine."

Rusty did indeed believe that. Despite his overall aversion to the human race, he had occasional moments where he wasn't a completely cynical bastard. As long as they made intelligent decisions (for example, not walking to the truck in the darkness) they'd be okay.

Now they had one more window to deal with. The headless bear filled the entire thing; nothing could squeeze past it. That said, Rusty didn't want to leave the bear wedged in there, even if he closed the bedroom door. Mia agreed with him, so they went in there with a board and used it to try and push the bear out of the window.

It wouldn't budge.

"Its legs are in the way," said Mia. "You need to cut them off even higher. Right at the shoulder."

Rusty refueled the chainsaw, started it up, and completely severed the bear's front legs. He kicked them into the corner of the room. Then they used the board again. The bear still wouldn't budge.

"Fuck," said Rusty.

"Fuck," Mia agreed.

"Push harder."

They pushed against the board until Rusty's feet slipped out from beneath him, though he spared himself the indignity of actually falling. "I know that it's one of God's creatures, but I really hate this bear. I mean on a deep personal level."

"Just keep sawing away," said Mia.

"I don't want to chainsaw it any more. I want to go to bed."

"I'll take over."

"No, no, I'm being a whiner. We're almost done."

Rusty revved up the chainsaw again and cut off a great big slab of the bear. That chunk landed on the bedroom floor, while the rest of the bear fell away from the window and landed on the ground outside. Rusty cut the indoor slab in half and shut off the chainsaw. A few minutes later, he and Mia had thrown all of the bear pieces out of the window with the rest of it. A few minutes after that, they'd boarded up the hole, once again leaving a tiny gap to see through.

To keep more wild animals from breaking through the glass, they boarded up the unbroken windows. Then they went around the cabin, double-checking their work. A bear charging at full speed could probably break through, but otherwise, the cabin was safe.

"Get some sleep," said Rusty. "I'll wake you up at sunrise."

"What makes you think I'll be able to sleep?"

"Try to at least doze. We've got a busy morning."

"Shouldn't you sleep, too?"

"I'm going to keep watch."

"We've got, what, three hours until daylight?" Mia asked. "You rest for an hour and a half and then I'll rest for an hour and a half."

"I guess we could both rest. We'd hear anything that was trying to get inside. It's not like keeping watch is going to improve our situation all that much."

"We should keep watch."

"I agree. I was just throwing out another option for no

real reason."

"Nudge me in ninety minutes," said Mia, lying down on the couch. "I won't be asleep."

A few minutes later, she was softly snoring. Rusty didn't blame her—it had been an exhausting night. He'd let her sleep until sunrise, even though she'd be pissed at him.

He got up to look through the windows. The floorboards were creaking now, so he stepped slowly and carefully. He peeked through the gap and saw nothing outside. Good. He sat back down on his recliner.

He waited another five minutes or so and then got up to check again. Still nothing out there that he could see.

After checking a third time, he decided that he should just scoot a chair over to the boarded-up window instead of walking across the room over and over. He picked up a wooden chair that Mia had made, placed it next to the window, and sat down. He peeked through the gap. Still nothing there.

That's right, stay away, he thought. *What happened to your buddies can happen to you. Let the scattered bear remains be a lesson to everything that lives in this forest. Rusty Moss will tear you motherfuckers to bits.*

He sat there for a while.

Suddenly it occurred to him that he wasn't sure how long he'd been sitting there. He hadn't fallen asleep, but he'd zoned out for a bit, and that could lead to falling asleep in this extremely well made chair. He stood up, crept across the creaking floor again, and got his alarm clock out of his bedroom. It was an old-fashioned wind-up model. Rusty almost never used it because he had a lifestyle that did not require him to get up at any specific time—the sun streaming through his window was his alarm clock. But the last thing he wanted was to wake up in a cabin surrounded by bears and discover that they'd missed their window of opportunity to escape, so he set the alarm for 6:30 AM and placed it on the floor next to the chair, just in case.

He peeked through the gap in the boards again. Still nothing dangerous that he could see.

Mia continued to snore.

Time was passing more slowly now that he could glance down and see what time it was. He wasn't looking forward to venturing out of the cabin, but he did wish that dawn would just get here already so he didn't have to sit here stressing out over it.

He kept waiting and peeking.

After about an hour, he thought he heard something scraping against the wood in his bedroom. He allowed himself about half a second to believe that it might be a figment of his paranoia-fueled imagination, but no, something was definitely scratching the wood.

He scooped up the flashlight and hurried into the bedroom. Whatever was out there was scratching on the boards over the window. Vigorously.

He went up to the window and peered through the gap. He could see movement but it was too dark to identify the next possible threat to his life. Rusty turned on the flashlight and shone it through the gap, catching a glimpse of gray and white fur.

The creature snarled, startling Rusty so badly that he almost dropped the flashlight.

"What is it?" asked Mia, startling him so badly that he *did* drop the flashlight.

"A wolf, I think," said Rusty.

The flashlight rolled out of his reach, so Mia picked it

up and gave it back to him. The creature continued to growl on the other side, and even though Rusty was very confident in the job they'd done boarding up the window, he still didn't want to stand too close to it.

Rusty didn't like this at all. A squirrel was ultimately harmless, and a bear would give plenty of advance notice if it charged at them through the woods, but a wolf was stealthy. If one of those leapt at them while they were running for the car, they were dead.

Mia left the bedroom, returning a moment later with the shotgun. By design, the gap was exactly big enough to fit the barrel through.

More scratching. This time against the wall, a few feet to the left.

Rusty took the shotgun from her, shoved the barrel through the gap, and tilted it down. The wolf didn't move as the metal pressed against it.

He squeezed the trigger.

The wolf let out a high-pitched squeal and Rusty heard it fall to the ground. Then he heard it get back up and resume aggressively scratching the boards.

He glanced back at Mia, who had her hand over her mouth as if to stifle a scream. He wanted to say something reassuring, but nothing came to mind, and it would be bullshit anyway.

Now something was scratching on the other wall. Not necessarily another wolf, but another *something*.

Rusty swiveled the barrel around, trying to make contact with the first wolf again. When the barrel smacked against it, he squeezed the trigger. He honestly couldn't tell if he'd hit it or not; the scratching didn't stop. He withdrew the shotgun and popped it open to reload it.

"I hear something in the front, too," said Mia, leaving the bedroom.

On one hand, it felt like a potentially fatal mistake to have waited in the cabin until it was surrounded. On the other hand, they'd be positively screwed if they ran into a pack of vicious wolves without the walls of the cabin to protect them. It didn't feel like it at the moment, but they'd made the right decision. He hoped.

He shoved two more shells into the shotgun, snapped it closed, and poked it through the gap again.

A couple of gunshots came from the living room.

"Did you get it?" Rusty called out.

"Yes."

"Did it do any good?"

"No."

Rusty cursed. He swiveled the shotgun barrel back and forth, squeezing the trigger when he smacked into the wolf. It yelped but didn't stop moving. He fired again. Another yelp. The scratching continued.

Mia fired her rifle a few more times.

"There are at least three of them in front," she announced.

They were just squandering their ammunition. If they were up against a whole pack of wild animals, they'd have to make every bullet count. Every shot had to be a skull-shattering hit, followed by another skull-shattering hit, and possibly even more than that, simply to take out one wolf.

He pulled the shotgun out from between the boards and went over to the doorway. "This isn't—"

"—a good idea?"

"Right. It's too dark."

"I can see the ones in front. I crippled one but I had to

shoot both of its front legs."

More scratching behind him. A third animal was at the bedroom wall. No, a fourth.

"All wolves?" Rusty asked.

Mia peeked through the gap. "Not anymore."

"What else?"

"Looks like a bobcat. I can see part of its skull."

"A bobcat wouldn't hunt with a pack of wolves."

"It's not a normal bobcat, then."

Rusty reloaded the shotgun. His optimism was gone.

CHAPTER ELEVEN

The good news was that the boards were staying put. And they had plenty of unused boards left in case they needed to reinforce their work.

The other good news was that, presumably, it would take an extremely long time for a pack of wolves to scratch their way through the walls of a cabin. They'd wear their claws down to bloody nubs before they actually got through.

That was pretty much it for the good news.

The bad news was that there were now a *lot* of wolves out there. A pack almost never got larger than fifteen, and this one seemed to have brought the entire extended family. Plus at least two bobcats. And Rusty and Mia were basing this estimate on what they could see in the night. There could be many more.

Rusty preferred the kinder, simpler time when he needed only to contend with two grizzly bears.

If these were animals that would die when you shot them in the fucking head like animals were supposed to, it was a situation that could be managed. They had more than enough rounds to take out a large pack of normal wolves circling the cabin. Counting up the rounds in the two ammo boxes and what was already in their six guns, they had about a hundred and twenty shots. Those could disappear pretty quickly when trying to incapacitate undead wolves.

After some discussion, they'd decided to conserve their firepower. They'd need the bullets much more desperately when they were running for the truck than when they were holed up inside the cabin. Which meant that their current plan was, "Keep themselves safe inside the cabin, and hope that things outside didn't continue to get worse." Rusty didn't like any plan where he wasn't actively taking charge of his own fate, but he liked it a lot more than embarking upon a three-mile run where he couldn't properly defend himself against fierce predators.

Getting some sleep, or even dozing, was a laughable idea at this point. Rusty wanted to start cleaning up the mess the bear had made in the kitchen and living room, just to give himself something productive to do, but Mia had vetoed the idea, insisting that they needed to conserve their energy. Rusty had negotiated his way down to sweeping things up but leaving the labor-intensive cleanup for later.

Frickin' bear, he thought as he swept broken dishes into a dustpan. It was going to cost a fortune to get this place back in shape.

"Are there more of them out there?" he asked Mia as she peeked out the window.

"Doesn't look like it."

"Are there fewer?"

"No."

"At least there aren't more."

"Yeah."

"That's me saying that the glass is half full."

"It doesn't suit you."

Rusty almost chuckled, then decided that he didn't feel like chuckling. He continued sweeping up the broken dishes. At least he wasn't the kind of guy to have an affinity for any particular coffee mug—the destruction of each of them pissed him off equally, but none had any sentimental value. They were just mugs.

Soon he'd cleaned up everything he could without violating Mia's "don't exert yourself so much that it slows us down when we're fleeing wolves later" rule. The kitchen and living room still looked like crap, but if the Queen of England showed up unexpectedly, he'd be less embarrassed than before.

Finally, it was dawn.

Now that they had some sunlight, Rusty and Mia were able to better gauge the situation outside. And it sucked just as much as it had in the darkness. Fourteen or fifteen wolves, about half of which had visible bones. Four bobcats; Rusty wasn't sure if the original two had been joined by two more, of if he simply hadn't been able to see the others at night. A few squirrels. At least there were no new bears.

Most of the animals were pacing around the yard. Some of them, including a bobcat whose face was ninety percent exposed skull, were on the porch.

"Did we make the right decision by waiting?" Rusty asked.

"I think so," said Mia. "Things look about the same out there. It would definitely be safer to make a run for it now than it would've been when it was dark out."

"Still not safe to make a run for it, though."

"No, not at all."

"I can't kill twenty of those things before they take me down."

"Me either."

"What kind of armor do we have?"

"We've got that vintage suit of knight's armor in the study."

"You don't have to be a smartass," said Rusty. "I meant protection. We can bulk up. Wear multiple layers of clothing. Strap on pieces of furniture."

Mia looked at him closely. "I can't tell if you're being serious."

"Of course I'm being serious!"

"You think we're going to make it past an entire pack of zombie wolves with a few extra shirts and a shield made out of a dresser drawer?"

"Well, what do you suggest?"

"Not going outside with the wolves."

"So we just sit here forever?"

Mia shook her head. "No, not forever. Until it makes more sense to go out there. How do you know we won't be rescued?"

"Who the hell is going to come out here and rescue us?"

"Mr. Olander?"

"We haven't seen him since your thirteenth birthday. He's a good guy, but he's not going to lead some rescue expedition. We're on our own. For twenty-five years I've been perfectly happy with the arrangement so I'm not going to whine about it now. If your plan is to sit on our thumbs until some lawyer shows up then I need to be the one making the plans."

"That wasn't my plan," said Mia. "I was just

mentioning it as a possibility. Yes, it's a remote possibility. Really remote. But I think we should look at really remote possibilities for rescue before we march out there to get devoured."

"It was stupid to even mention it."

"Fine."

Rusty wanted to kick something, but he'd just cleaned the place up, so he sighed instead. "Shit, I'm sorry. We're not supposed to be at each other's throats at a time like this. I don't think I need to explain that my stress level is pretty high right now."

"Mine too. So, we got the bickering out of our system. Now we can work together in perfect harmony until we get out of this nightmare."

Rusty walked over and peeked out the front window.

"Are all the wolves still there?" Mia asked.

"Yeah."

"At least they aren't actively trying to get—" Mia was interrupted by a loud scratching from her bedroom window. "Never mind."

They both looked up as something scurried across the roof.

"I think that was a squirrel," said Rusty.

Something else scurried across the roof.

"I think that was another squirrel."

Nothing else scurried. Two squirrels. No big deal. They might not even be zombie squirrels.

"I apologize for making fun of you about the armor," said Mia. "It's not a completely stupid idea if you really think about it. We've got plenty of boards and duct tape. If we taped strips of wood to our arms and chest it would help a *little*, right?"

Rusty nodded. "If it makes us ten percent less likely to

get torn to shreds, it's worth it."

"Let's do it."

The table saw was in the shed, but they had a couple of hacksaws in the cabin. This wasn't going to be anything elaborate; in fact, Mia and Rusty were going to look and feel ridiculous. And it would weigh them down enough to prevent them from taking the three miles at a sprint. But if it provided sufficient protection to get in a good swipe with the chainsaw before any particular wolf could mangle them, it might be the secret to their survival.

The wolves continued to claw at the boarded-up windows while Rusty and Mia sawed the wood into properly measured pieces. Rusty didn't like that the animals were focusing all of their attention on the windows. The bears had randomly scraped at the walls, but the wolves were concentrating on the weakest part of the cabin. No, they weren't going to be able to break through; still, Rusty didn't appreciate the way they were demonstrating intelligence.

"Do you think we could trap them?" Mia asked.

"How?"

"Rope. We lay a noose out on the porch. When a wolf steps into it, we pull it tight."

"All of our rope is in the shed."

"Correct. We'd have to make another visit to the shed."

Rusty shrugged. "Could work, I guess."

"I'm not suggesting it as a Plan A. I'm saying that if we find ourselves stuck here for a while, like days or weeks, it could be a way of gradually lowering the numbers."

"I'm not planning to be stuck here days or weeks."

"Neither am I," said Mia. "But if we step outside and

all of the wolves suddenly charge at us at once, we should probably go back inside."

Rusty placed a wooden strip over his forearm, double-checking the length. It had been cut and measured perfectly, of course. "We've got enough food to last a few weeks. If we do have to abandon the escape plan, we should be okay for quite a while, but I'd rather deal with twenty zombie animals surrounding the cabin now than five hundred zombie animals surrounding the cabin in a month."

"I can't argue that," said Mia. "I guess it just surprises me that you want to leave. I would've expected you to have a 'No goddamn zombie animals are going to drive me out of my home' attitude."

"I don't want to die. And I especially don't want you to die. I tried to be optimistic, and it didn't work, so now I believe that things are going to continue to get worse. Therefore, we need to get the hell out of here as soon as we can. This is totally in line with my world view."

Mia nodded. "We'll make it. I'm confident that all twenty of them won't pounce on us as soon as we step outside. We've got protection, we've got guns, we've got an axe, and we've got a chainsaw. We'll be fine."

"Look me in the eye when you say that," Rusty told her.

Mia looked him in the eye. "Do you want me to say the whole thing again?"

"Nah, that's all right." Rusty surveyed the strips of wood they'd cut. "We've got all of them. Ready to start taping them on?"

"Yeah." Mia went into the kitchen and retrieved the roll of duct tape from underneath the sink. As she returned, she glanced over at the living room window, where a wolf was aggressively scratching. "We're making the right decision," she said. "Even if they can't get in, listening to them constantly *trying* to get in would drive me insane."

"Me too," said Rusty. "Do you want to tape or be taped first?"

"I'll tape."

Rusty held out his left arm. Mia placed the first strip of wood on his forearm and wrapped a piece of tape around it. She placed the second strip and wrapped the tape around both pieces. Mia worked quickly and soon Rusty's entire arm was covered, wrist to shoulder, except for the joint.

"How does it feel?" she asked.

Rusty bent his arm at the elbow. "Heavy."

"Too heavy?"

"No, it's fine. When one of those things has my arm in its jaws, I'll be glad it's heavy. I think this is going to work."

They kept going. As wolves continued to claw at the windows, Mia duct-taped strips of wood to Rusty's body. Eventually he was covered except for his hands, feet, and head. His boots would protect his feet, and he'd put on thick gloves after he armored up Mia.

He walked around the living room, flexing his arms and legs. This was definitely going to slow him down, but it wasn't restricting his radius of movement, and, yeah, he thought that if a wolf was trying to tear his stomach open, he could slice it in half with his chainsaw before it succeeded.

Rusty began the process on Mia. She made several comments about wanting to paint her armor to make it more intimidating, and had to point out to Rusty that she was joking when he questioned whether they had time for such a thing.

"Sorry," he said. "Stress relief humor isn't working for me right now."

Something bashed into the living room window, hard.

Rusty and Mia both glanced over. Another bash. The boards held.

"What the hell is that?" Rusty asked, walking over there and peeking through the gap.

A wolf, half of its face already crushed, was running toward the window. It smashed into the boards, rattling them. It walked back down the stairs, staggering a bit, then turned around and raced at the window yet again. The impact was worse on its skull than the wood, and its left eye now protruded from the socket.

It stumbled off the porch, got another running start, and sprinted at the window. None of the boards broke or fell off, but one of them was coming loose on the edge.

The wolf flopped onto its side.

Another wolf took its place. It charged at the window, crashing into it at full speed.

The boards were designed to withstand efforts to claw through them. They were not designed to withstand suicidal wolves smashing into them.

The loose board fell to the floor. The nails were still imbedded in it, so Rusty picked up a hammer and hurriedly pounded it back into place.

Mia peeked through the gap just as the wolf smashed into the boards again.

Several other wolves were standing in the front yard, watching, as if waiting their turn.

Mia looked at Rusty. She didn't need to say, "The boards aren't going to hold!" It was very much understood by both of them.

"Let's give it another layer as fast as we can," said Rusty. "We at least need to keep them out long enough for me to finish up your armor."

Rusty grabbed a board and began to nail it diagonally across the others. Mia did the same thing. Her breath was coming so quickly that Rusty thought she might be close to hyperventilating, but as long as her hands weren't trembling so badly that she dropped the hammer and nails, all was not yet lost. Let the wolves splatter themselves. Fewer to deal with when it was time to flee the cabin.

Two wolves smashed into the boards, one right after the other. So much for the comforting idea that at least they were attacking one at a time.

Now Rusty wished they'd brought in more boards. It had seemed like plenty before. They had enough to do another full layer over the living room window, and the strips he still needed to duct tape to Mia, and then the two boards they'd use to give the truck traction to get out of the mud and that would be pretty much it for the wood.

A wolf let out a loud yip as it made a particularly brutal impact on the boards. Rusty's sympathy for the creatures of the forest had significantly diminished since the time he felt kind of bad for the grizzly bears, but he still felt a tinge of regret that the wolves were suffering like this. Though he didn't know what was causing their behavior, it wasn't any more their fault than if they were rabid dogs.

They finished putting up the second layer of boards. Rusty hoped the barricade would survive long enough for him to armor up Mia but he had very serious doubts.

They should've done her before him.

Mia extended her arm and Rusty began to tape the strips of wood to it, working quickly but efficiently. Mia flinched every time a wolf smashed into the window.

A board dropped to the floor.

"It's gonna be okay," Rusty assured her. "You're almost done." She wasn't anywhere close to being done, but Mia nodded as if pretending to be soothed.

Another board popped loose but didn't fall.

That same board broke a moment later. It didn't come all the way apart but the center of it splintered. It wouldn't make it through another hit.

Rusty's cynicism was proven correct as the board broke in half and a snarling wolf shoved its head through the gap.

CHAPTER TWELVE

Rusty grabbed the axe and lopped off the wolf's head with one swing. He was getting good at this. The head dropped to the floor, landing stump-down. The wolf soundlessly opened and closed its mouth, trying unsuccessfully to bite Rusty's foot.

Another wolf ran for the window. Rusty swung the axe like a baseball bat, striking the wolf in the mouth just as its face came through, shattering its front teeth and chopping off the entire top half of its head. It pulled the bottom half of its head out of the gap, whimpering.

A third wolf smashed into the window, knocking off another board. Rusty slashed at it with the axe, getting it in the shoulder but not effectively. A fourth wolf stuck its head into the gap.

Outside, a few of the wolves began howling.

Mia ran into the kitchen as Rusty kept swinging the axe. A wolf clamped its jaws upon his arm, and he knew it would've torn off a huge chunk of flesh if not for the strips of wood. He slammed the axe blade into its back and it released its grip.

He wrenched the blade free. There was, of course, no blood on the steel. The wolf had not run off yelping, like any reasonable mammal would after taking an axe to the back, and Rusty swung the axe at its neck. This time it only went about three quarters of the way through. Its head flopped forward. It continued trying to bite Rusty.

Mia returned to the window with a can of lighter fluid and some matches. "Great idea," he told her.

Rusty lopped off the wolf's head and kicked it out of the way as Mia doused the other wolf with fluid. Another wolf took the spot of the just-decapitated one, and Mia sprayed it as well. Then she dropped the can on the floor and struck a match.

The match burst into flame, then immediately went out.

She struck another match, which did the same thing. If they survived long enough to purchase more supplies, Rusty would buy more expensive matches.

The third match stayed lit long enough for her to toss it onto one of the wolves.

Its fur ignited right away, and the fire immediately spread to the wolf next to it. The first wolf pulled away from the window, thrashing around in pain and terror. The second wolf also thrashed around in pain and terror, but it moved in the opposite direction, leaping all the way into the cabin. This was not at *all* what Rusty had expected when he'd told Mia that it was a great idea. Wolves on fire were supposed to run away!

Rusty swung the axe at it. The panicked wolf sprinted past him and the blade struck its tail without severing it. The wolf began to run in circles as the flames grew more intense. The smell of burnt fur filled the cabin.

It was good that the wolf was freaking out too much

to attack them, but a flaming wolf was not something they wanted running around their home.

Rusty glanced out the window. The first wolf was also running in circles, and a bobcat and another wolf got the hell out of its way. So perhaps a torch would help keep him and Mia safe when it was finally time to venture outside.

The knowledge that the undead animals were scared of fire provided about half a second of comfort, before it became necessary to address the issue of a wolf that was coming very close to the many flammable items in the cabin. Rusty went after it with the axe. A wolf and a bobcat simultaneously appeared at the window, and Mia tried to beat them away with a board.

Rusty took a vicious downward swing at the wolf. Missed by a lot. The blade went deep into the floorboards, and it took a few tries to pry it out, during which time the wolf ran into his bedroom.

He followed it, hoping it wouldn't jump on his bed.

The wolf leapt onto his bed.

Was it moving with blind panic, or purposely trying to spread the flames? If Rusty was engulfed in an inferno, he wouldn't be thinking coherently about anything, but why would the wolf have jumped up there if not to set fire to the blankets?

He was probably attributing too much intelligence to the beast. A wolf with plenty of time to ponder would not reach the conclusion that blankets and sheets were more combustible, and thus a wolf would not come up with that idea while its flesh was sizzling. There was no conscious reasoning behind the fact that the goddamn wolf was rolling around on his bed, setting fire to his blankets.

Rusty took another swing at the wolf with the axe. The wolf twisted its head out of the way at the last moment, so the axe blade struck the mattress instead. Then the axe bounced back up, startling Rusty so badly that he almost lost his grip. Fortunately, it did not slip out of his hands and imbed itself into his skull. He would not have handled this as well as the zombie animals.

Finally, he chopped its head off, unevenly. Four more whacks with the axe and the poor thing was legless. Now it was still burning but wouldn't be running around setting more fires. All of the fur on its head had burnt away, though the skull was still aflame, looking about as demonic as anything Rusty had ever seen in real life, paintings, or nightmares.

He hurried out of the bedroom. Mia smacked a bobcat in the face with a board. A couple of sharp teeth dropped to the floor, but the bobcat continued trying to squirm through the window.

Rusty ran into the kitchen to grab the fire extinguisher, then hesitated. Where *was* the fire extinguisher? He knew they had one, but he hadn't needed to use it the entire time he'd lived in the cabin. He'd never started an unwanted fire. Where the hell was it?

Mia bashed the bobcat again. Its face was a smushed up mess, but it didn't seem to mind. Mia smacked the wolf that was next to it, and it also was clearly more interested in trying to fight its way into the cabin than avoiding getting repeatedly hit by a plank of wood.

There. By the refrigerator. Rusty picked up the fire extinguisher and returned to his bedroom, which was filled with so much smoke that he could barely see the floor. Since there was a wolf head on the floor, he stepped carefully, not wanting to add "missing a few toes" to the challenges facing them during the trip to the truck.

The bed was completely engulfed in flames, and the fire seemed to be spreading. Rusty set down the axe, since he needed both hands to operate the fire extinguisher.

"One got in!" Mia shouted.

Rusty heard footsteps moving toward him. He spun around and saw a wolf, face misshapen from Mia's beating, running for the doorway to the bedroom. He really wished he hadn't put down the axe. It was as if every move he made, even something as obvious as "I'd better put out the fire," was turning out to be the wrong one.

The wolf snarled and leapt at him.

Rusty instinctively held his arm over his face.

The wolf knocked him to the floor. Rusty's head struck the floorboards and for an instant his vision went black. His vision returned to the blurred sight of the wolf's jaws open wide and coming at his throat.

He slammed the fire extinguisher into the side of the wolf's head, knocking its jaws away from their target. Some drool splattered onto his chin. The wolf raked its claws over his chest, an act which would have created several red streaks were it not for the protective strips of wood. Rusty coughed from the smoke and then bashed the wolf's head again. It bit the extinguisher then let it go.

His eyes were watering so badly that he could barely see anything. Fortunately, the wolf was not difficult to locate, since it was right on top of him. Rusty struggled with the fire extinguisher for a moment, then finally blasted it directly into the wolf's face. It seemed to enjoy this much less than actually having the metal canister slam into its head. It scampered off Rusty and smacked right into the bed.

Its fur immediately caught on fire. Then it fled the bedroom.

Rusty sat up. He wanted to shout out a warning to Mia but he couldn't stop coughing. He got to his feet and staggered out of the bedroom just in time to see Mia swing the board at the running wolf, hitting it so hard that its neck snapped. The wolf changed course and slammed into the wall. Mia returned her attention to fighting off the animals that were trying to get inside.

Rusty blasted the wolf with the fire extinguisher so that it couldn't run around starting new fires, then stepped back into his bedroom. He didn't care about saving the cabin, but if the whole thing caught on fire they'd have to abandon it no matter how dangerous things were outside. So he went back into his bedroom and sprayed at the flames with the fire extinguisher. His bed was an inferno and his bookshelf and clothes dresser were also on fire, and it was quickly evident that the extinguisher was not designed for a job of this scope. The cabin was history.

He really wished he'd insisted that Mia's "armor" go on first. The cabin had seemed secure. There'd been no reason to think the clock was ticking this rapidly.

He left the bedroom, shutting the door behind him to hopefully keep the flames from spreading to the rest of the cabin quite as fast. The wolf, smoke billowing from its burnt flesh, ran at Mia, but its sense of direction was impacted by the way its head lolled off to the side, and Mia was able to bash it once again with the board. This time the board split in half.

Rusty could not imagine how bad it must hurt to have

severely burnt skin get whacked hard with a board. And yet the wolf made another attempt to get at Mia. A feeble, pathetic attempt, but it still *tried*.

"How are things in the bedroom?" Mia asked, smacking a bobcat with what remained of the board.

"Apocalyptic. We need to leave as soon as we can." Rusty dropped the fire extinguisher. He'd hoped to conserve gasoline in case they were in an even shittier situation later, but that wasn't really an option anymore. It was time again for the chainsaw.

He glanced around, found the chainsaw, and hurried over to pick it up. He hated to admit that he was already getting kind of tired from the extra weight of the wood taped to his body—not a good sign.

"I'll take the chainsaw and the axe," he said, though he couldn't use either of them effectively if he was carrying both. They had a pair of backpacks ready, and the axe would have to go in there (handle protruding from the top) until it was needed. The backpacks also had the pistols and ammunition, along with a couple of bottles of water each. The rifles had shoulder straps.

Technically, they didn't *need* the boards to get the truck out of the mud. They could use sticks or rocks they gathered at the scene, or even place the truck's floor mats behind the back tires to give them traction. But it wouldn't be as quick and easy as using actual boards, and "quick and easy" might mean the difference between life and death. More importantly, Mia was getting good at using the boards as weapons, though hopefully she wouldn't break them against any wolves before they reached the truck, or if that advice was annoyingly obvious.

The shotgun would have to stay behind. Rusty hated

to leave it, but they couldn't bring everything.

"Guard the window," Mia told him.

Rusty pulled the cord and started the chainsaw. He waved the whirring blade over the large gap in the boards, immediately lopping off a bobcat's front paw. This didn't remove its desire to get inside and eat them or whatever it wanted to do, of course, so Rusty was able to saw it into a couple more pieces as it tried to scramble into the living room.

Honestly, this was working pretty well. If the rest of the animals outside kept trying to get in through this window, he and Mia could probably subdue them one or two at a time, like a crowd of bad guys in an old martial arts movie. They just needed the burning cabin not to collapse upon them first.

The smoke was becoming an issue. Rusty's eyes were starting to sting and he couldn't defend himself against undead creatures if he couldn't see properly. He slammed the chainsaw blade directly between a wolf's eyes, spraying fur and brain matter all over.

There were still plenty of animals surrounding the cabin. Excluding the need to not catch fire or perish of smoke inhalation, this was a terrible time to abandon their home.

Mia returned to the window, carrying but not wearing her backpack. "How long does it take a cabin to burn down?" she asked.

"Not long. We can't carry the shotgun, so we should just use up all of the ammunition. Do as much damage to these things as possible before we're forced outside with them."

Mia nodded and went to retrieve the weapon. While she did that, Rusty sliced off a wolf's snout, leaving only the back of its jaw to snap open and closed. A squirrel leapt over the blade, landed on the floor, and scampered up Rusty's leg. He swung the chainsaw blade at it and missed. Then he scolded himself for coming within a couple of inches of hitting his own leg with a chainsaw. It was important not to do things like that.

The squirrel ran up Rusty's back. He let go of the chainsaw with his right hand and reached behind his back to swipe off the squirrel with his left. He winced in pain as its tiny teeth clamped down on the back of his neck.

Mia knocked the squirrel off his shoulder with the barrel of the shotgun. It struck the floor and immediately ran at her. She slammed her foot down upon it. Rusty knew he couldn't actually hear the loud *crunch* over the chainsaw, but he certainly imagined it. The squirrel, spine broken, rolled on its side, frantically squirming.

Rusty slashed at a wolf with the chainsaw blade. He had to stay focused. They knew absolutely nothing about how these creatures worked, and so a bite might be nothing more than an ordinary squirrel bite. It didn't hurt that bad. It was nothing to worry about. And if it turned out that it *was* something to worry about, they could at least save the worrying for later. They had more than enough problems to deal with right now.

Mia shoved the barrel of the shotgun through the gap in the boards. A wolf chomped down on the end of it. Though they wouldn't argue that it was a good thing that all of these animals were frantically trying to get inside, it was conducive to more accurate shots.

She squeezed the trigger. Much of the wolf's head disappeared.

She squeezed the trigger again, putting a significant hole in the wolf behind it.

While Mia reloaded, Rusty kept waving the chainsaw and tried not to think about the bite on his neck.

Mia fired off two more shots, both going point blank into wolves. They all kept moving, but they had less body mass with which to pose a threat.

Even with its broken back, that frickin' squirrel was crawling toward Rusty. He knelt down and sawed it in half, and then into quarters. He would've liked to saw it into eighths or even sixteenths, but there were much larger, more dangerous animals trying to get into the cabin that required attention.

Rusty glanced back for a moment. Flames were visible underneath his bedroom door.

Mia reloaded and fired off two more shots.

It was starting to get uncomfortably hot in the cabin.

Mia shouted something at Rusty that he couldn't hear. He shut off the chainsaw.

"Throw some burning wood at them," she said. "Or burning whatever."

That was a good idea. Rusty went over to the bedroom door, hoping his gloves were sufficient protection against the hot knob. They were. As he opened the door, a massive amount of smoke billowed out. He couldn't see in there well enough to grab a burning object, so he picked up a couch cushion and held it in the flames until it caught on fire. Then he returned to the window.

Mia shot two more wolves, then moved out of the way as Rusty tossed the burning cushion out the window. The animals backed away from it. They didn't run off the porch, but they left plenty of room between themselves and the fire.

It was working!

Rusty grabbed the last two cushions. He set them on

fire then tossed them out the window, one at a time, trying to land them away from each other to cover more territory on the porch. One of the wolves backed down the stairs.

Now the trick was to scare away the animals with fire without trapping themselves inside a burning cabin. Being burned alive was quite a bit more agonizing than being mauled by teeth and claws, or so Rusty had been led to believe. He hoped to never acquire first-hand information on either method.

Rusty placed a couple of thin boards halfway into the bedroom. He'd use them as torches when it became time to flee, which was going to happen any minute now. Then he grabbed a jacket, set it on fire, and flung it out the window.

Mia fired two more shots. "That's it for the shotgun ammo," she said. "But I made every shot count."

"Perfect. Let's get the rifles."

Mia tossed the shotgun aside and they each picked up a rifle and slung it over their back. It felt really heavy. Rusty wondered if he might have to dump some of his weaponry before their hike was over.

He hurriedly put both the axe and the chainsaw in his backpack. Hopefully he'd never have to access them—he could just keep the predators away with fire. He put the backpack on over the rifle. Oh yeah, the journey to the truck was going to suck in a big way. But at least they might survive for longer than twelve seconds.

Mia put on her backpack as well. They gave each other a quick nod, like warriors about to go into battle where the odds were overwhelmingly against them. This would've been a good time for a hug, though Rusty wasn't much of a hugger. However, they were weighed down and a little off-balance and an "I hope we don't die" hug might topple one or both of them over.

Should he tell her he loved her? It wasn't unheard of him to speak those words, but it wasn't normal, either. It might make things awkward and put too much of an emphasis on the idea that they might be moments away from a horrific, gruesome death. Then again, if he found himself lying on the ground, blood spurting from six different wounds, a bobcat gnawing on the stump that used to be his left arm, he'd regret not saying something nice to Mia before their tragic demise. He kind of hoped she'd say it first.

"I love you, Uncle Rusty," said Mia.

"I love you, too," he said, coughing.

"I think we need more fire out there."

"Okay."

They set some more of their possessions on fire and tossed them out the window. By the time they were done, they'd cleared the front porch of zombie animals, though several of them were still lurking nearby.

Rusty went to get the thin boards, which were burning on the ends. Mia picked up the boards they'd use to (hopefully) free the truck.

"You ready?" he asked.

"No."

"Me either."

"Let's go."

They climbed out the living room window.

CHAPTER THIRTEEN

Rusty held a burning board in each hand. Suddenly the torches seemed kind of pathetic, as if he were trying to frighten off the animals with a cigarette lighter. Still, they'd been on the front porch for nearly three full seconds and no zombie wolves had charged at them yet.

They carefully stepped around the many fires, some of which came from headless wolves that were now burning, and then went down the two stairs. They no longer had the protection of the cabin walls. One advantage to the cabin being on fire was that Rusty couldn't second-guess their decision to leave. Since they did not want to become charred skeletons, there was no question that it was the correct plan of action. It was just as well that the cabin was going to burn to the ground; they'd never get the smell of burnt fur out of the place anyway.

Rusty took a quick inventory of the dangers surrounding them. Maybe nine or ten wolves, though at least half of them were injured. The one favoring its left front paw was still a threat, while the one with no remaining eyes was probably not going to cause them any problems. Two of the four bobcats remained mobile. So the situation was bad—very, very bad—but not as bad as it had been before they made use of the shotgun, axe, and chainsaw.

The animals were keeping their distance, in that their jaws were not currently within biting range of Rusty and Mia's throats. Using any other measure, they were too fucking close. Rusty swung the torches in front of him, which was enough to keep the animals out of torch range but not much further.

"Get the hell out of here," he told them, as if the command might cause the undead creatures to reconsider their choices.

Rusty lunged at the closest wolf with the torch. The flames got close enough to sear its snout a bit, yet the wolf didn't flee. Mia waved her boards in an effort to be menacing; it was enough to keep the animals out of range of getting whacked, but just barely.

Rusty took a step forward. The closest wolf growled. Rusty took a step backward.

"This isn't working," he told Mia, as if she'd been under the impression that everything had been working out in a perfectly delightful manner. He'd been saying a lot of unnecessary shit since they'd left the cabin.

"Maybe the chainsaw is better than the fire," said Mia.

A couple of the other wolves began to growl as well. But, again, they weren't pouncing and trying to tear the humans apart. As long as there was an element of "Perhaps we shouldn't be so hasty in devouring our prey" in their behavior, Rusty felt that his and Mia's saga might have a happy ending.

He didn't want to switch out the torch for the chainsaw quite yet. Yes, the chainsaw was much better at grinding up their faces, but the animals hadn't demonstrated any actual fear of it. The torch was keeping them away. Not *far* away, but away. If they lost their fear and all decided to charge at once, the chainsaw wasn't going to extend his life by more than a few extra seconds, and those extra seconds would be filled with terror and pain and quite honestly wouldn't be worth living.

A wolf got too close to Mia and she lightly bopped it in the face with a board. Another wolf snapped at Rusty's torch. Several of the wolves were growling now. None of them seemed like they had any immediate plans to step aside and let Rusty and Mia pass.

Rusty really, really wished his cabin wasn't on fire. That would be so wonderful right now.

He and Mia stepped back onto the porch. The animals didn't follow.

"Are we fucked?" asked Mia.

Rusty shook his head. "We'll figure something out."

Granted, they'd spent quite a bit of time waiting for daylight and hadn't come up with a more elaborate plan than heavily arming themselves. Presumably there was some sort of brilliant scheme that could get them out of this mess, but Rusty had no idea what it was. He just figured at some point he'd have to whip out the chainsaw and start severing things.

Almost all of the wolves had walked to the edge of the porch, blocking the steps.

"At least they're..." Rusty trailed off, fear making him completely forget what he was going to say. He wasn't even sure if it had been a joke or not.

The porch was not going to be a semi-safe place to

stand for very much longer. The wood was burning in several spots and though the foundation seemed solid, Rusty couldn't tell what was happening underneath and the whole thing could collapse with very little warning. One of them would probably have caught on fire before that, but still, they needed to be aware of the porch stability while they tried to work out an escape plan.

Mia didn't ask him to complete his sentence. She seemed to realize it was a comment that his brain had erased.

"They're too scared of the fire to come up here with us," said Mia. "But they're staying right on the edge. That means we can hack them up some more."

She was correct. Rusty set down his torches. He reached behind him, unzipped the top of the backpack, and tugged on the axe handle. The axe wouldn't come free; it was wedged against something, probably the chainsaw. He tugged more vigorously. It remained stuck. Shoving everything into the backpack in a rushed panic apparently had a downside.

This was the kind of thing that would impede his ability to whip out a weapon and fire off a snappy one-liner—that and not being able to think of a snappy one-liner. Fortunately, the animals were still staying away from the fire, so this setback was embarrassing but not yet fatal.

He took off the backpack and got the axe out of it. He handed it to Mia, who'd set her boards down where they wouldn't catch on fire, at least for the next couple of minutes. Then he removed the chainsaw.

He tugged the cord. The chainsaw didn't start.

He tugged it again. The chainsaw didn't start.

He cursed and tugged it a third time. The chainsaw

sputtered but didn't start.

Mia slammed the axe into the skull of a wolf.

Rusty set the chainsaw down so that he could pull the cord with both hands. No way was it out of gasoline already. It was just being a dick.

The axe would not come out of the wolf's skull. Mia yanked on it repeatedly, but all she was doing was dragging the wolf up the steps. Rusty took a quick break from his chainsaw predicament to kick the wolf in the face as hard as he could. The axe popped free. The wolf continued to snarl. Rusty realized that he was getting used to the idea that a wolf could take an axe to the brain and still maintain all of its motor functions. Better to accept the impossible than to succumb to the black void of madness, he supposed.

Mia took another swing at the wolf, lopping off one of its ears. A squirrel grabbed the ear in its mouth and ran off with it, whether for a meal, blanket, or souvenir, Rusty couldn't be certain. A different wolf snapped up the squirrel, clamping its jaws tightly down on the rodent's writhing body, then vigorously shook its head back and forth. The squirrel dropped the ear. The wolf bit down even harder. Blood sprayed upon its muzzle, then it let the squirrel fall to the ground, missing a good-sized chunk of its torso. The wolf licked its chops and then chewed. The one-eared wolf gobbled down the rest of the squirrel.

Though this ten-second display of carnage was not a pleasant sight, the victim was clearly a regular living squirrel. That meant that whatever was creating the zombie animals had not impacted every single animal in the forest. It wasn't a *hugely* comforting thought, but right now Rusty would take whatever morsel of hope the universe was willing to toss at him.

Meanwhile, the fire was getting really frickin' hot.

He knelt down and tugged the cord. The chainsaw didn't start.

He tugged it again. The chainsaw didn't start.

Mia did not ask if he needed help. In pretty much any other set of circumstances, he would have turned her down and felt a mild blow to his male pride, but right now he did kind of want help starting the goddamn chainsaw. He wondered if he'd have to use it as a bludgeoning weapon instead.

Rusty couldn't keep squandering time and energy on this thing. They had other weapons; they simply weren't as effective and personally satisfying as the chainsaw. He gave the cord one last half-hearted tug...and of course it roared to life.

He picked it up with both hands. There was a sudden burst of adrenaline. The energy didn't quite reach his brain, since the only thing he could think of to say was, "That's right, you bastards, my chainsaw is working again!" and he elected not to say that out loud. It was lame and the chainsaw noise would drown it out anyway.

Mia slammed the axe into another wolf's skull. Before she'd finished wrenching out the blade, Rusty sawed off its head. The headless body ran up the steps and toward the open window to the cabin, though it veered off-course, smacked into the wall instead, and flopped onto a burning part of the floor.

Rusty thrust the whirring blade at another wolf. He missed and it snapped at his hand. Fortunately, it missed as well—Rusty's gloves weren't going to offer much protection against getting his hand bitten off. He swung the chainsaw at it again. The wolf somehow dodged this attack as well. But then Mia struck it in the side with the axe, and the wolf didn't dodge Rusty's next chainsaw swing.

With the axe and the chainsaw, Rusty and Mia made a pretty damn good team.

Sure, they were still surrounded by undead animals and trapped on a burning front porch. But it was starting to feel as if they might be able to significantly reduce the zombie wolf population before he and Mia died a horrible death in a fire.

They exchanged a glance, and the message was clear: *let's fuck these things up.*

Rusty and Mia went absolutely batshit insane with their respective weapons. Not to the point where one of them might accidentally chop/saw a limb off the other, but to the point where pieces of wolves and bobcats literally flew into the air. Rusty even let out a battle cry. None of the animals worked up the courage to join them on the porch—excluding the headless one that was still burning and slowly dragging itself across the floor—but they also didn't flee the scene. So it put Rusty and Mia in a nice position to be able to hack them apart.

There were no stunning, impressive moves. Nothing where Rusty decapitated two wolves with one swing, or where Mia chopped an entire wolf in half, lengthwise. But as they stood there, bodies covered in sweat, eyes watering from the smoke, skin hurting from the heat, they were doing some *serious* damage to these creatures.

Chunks of wolf and bobcat were scattered all over. Most of the pieces were still moving, but they wouldn't be a threat unless accidentally stepped upon.

Rusty's arms were starting to ache from swinging the heavy chainsaw around. The wooden armor also wasn't helping his fatigue, but he didn't regret it, especially when a wolf managed to slash its paw diagonally across his chest. As with the wolf from before, this tore open his shirt but not his flesh.

A squirrel leapt onto his pants. Mia made a move with the axe but Rusty waved her away. It took a few tries, but he finally got it with the chainsaw. The two halves of its body fell, spilling innards but no blood.

Unfortunately, the fire was simply getting too intense. They weren't going to be able to stay on the porch much longer, and though they'd dismembered plenty of wildlife, there were still four wolves and a bobcat left in the immediate area. They could definitely finish them off one-by-one, but five of them pouncing at once was going to be a real problem.

Mia wiped some perspiration off her forehead and said something that Rusty couldn't hear. He pointed to his ear. She mouthed her words carefully: *I need to go.*

Rusty nodded. Shit. Five more minutes and it would be safe. But he was pretty close to having to jump off the porch himself—five more minutes simply was not going to happen.

He mouthed back: *Okay.*

Then he let out a yelp as blistering pain shot through his legs.

Though the fire had been painful throughout the front porch wolf massacre, this was infinitely worse. He'd occasionally glanced behind him, but all of the danger was in front, and the chainsaw was masking all other noises. So he hadn't noticed that the headless burning wolf had somehow dragged itself directly behind him, and then right into the back of his legs.

The sudden pain caused him to lose his balance.

Rusty fell on his ass. The chainsaw, fortunately, landed right next to him and not on his groin. The motor shut off.

Normally this would simply be embarrassing, something where he'd sheepishly get back to his feet and hope that Mia showed some mercy when she made fun of him. In this case, there was a burning wolf directly underneath his ass. Any sense of embarrassment was far outweighed by landing on a soft but flaming object.

He screamed.

He frantically rolled over, and an exposed rib bone jabbed against his leg. Thank God for the wood taped there—otherwise it would've broken the skin for sure and possibly plunged in deep. That was only a minor solace. He rolled completely off the wolf, landing on the porch floor. Rusty was still on fire.

He couldn't be sure how expansive the flames were, but the pain was unreal. *Stop, drop, and roll* immediately popped into his mind in the voice of his second-grade teacher, Mrs. Janzing, who was a fire safety enthusiast to the point where, in retrospect, she might have been over-compensating for pyromania. He'd already stopped, the dropping was involuntary, and he was in the midst of the rolling process. Unfortunately, there were fires all over the porch. Almost nowhere to roll.

Mia screamed and knelt down next to him. "Roll over!" she shouted. "Roll over!"

Rusty rolled onto his stomach. Mia began to frantically smack at the flames. He had no idea what she was using, hopefully not her bare hands.

"Roll back! Roll back!"

She shoved Rusty onto his back. Then she pulled him onto his stomach again.

"Keep doing that!"

Rusty obliged while Mia hurriedly removed her backpack and dropped it onto the deck. She rifled through the contents and pulled out a bottle of water. Rusty kept rolling back and forth as she unscrewed the cap. He could tell that he was still on fire. How badly? Third-degree burns? Would he ever walk again?

"Okay, now stop!" she said.

She poured the water onto his legs. Rusty heard the hiss of the water instantly turning to vapor. She poured out the complete contents of the bottle, shook out the last few drops, and tossed the bottle aside. "You're out," she informed him.

He didn't *feel* like the flames were out—it felt like a hot iron was pressed tightly against his legs and buttocks—but he'd trust her. If it only took one bottle of water to extinguish the fire, maybe it hadn't been that bad. Touching your finger to a hot stove for half a second caused excruciating pain, so perhaps his legs weren't burnt down to the charred bone.

At some point in the extremely near future he'd probably have to tell Mia to leave him behind and save herself. He'd give it another thirty seconds or so. He didn't want to jump straight to that conversation.

Rusty sat up. The front of his pants was intact. He bent his knees; it was nice to discover that he could still bend his knees. He reached underneath his leg and touched wood.

He'd caught on fire and it had hurt like hell, but the wood had more or less protected him. Taping those boards all over him had seemed kind of dumb when they were doing it, but right now he was confident that it was the best idea his niece had ever come up with in the entirety of her nearly eighteen years of life.

Oh, his legs still hurt, and he was positive that they were covered in blisters, but he didn't think he'd have to order her to abandon him to be eaten by the zombie wolves. This came as a relief.

The sense of relief was short-lived. Right before his fall, his attention had been occupied by the fact that they were trapped on a burning front porch with four wolves and a bobcat still wanting to prey upon them. This situation hadn't changed. They were in exactly the same predicament as before, except that the fires had more time to grow, he'd have even more difficulty running, and he might not be able to get the chainsaw started again.

Mia helped him to his feet. He wobbled a bit but remained upright.

Mia put her backpack on and handed him the axe. "I'll trade you," she said.

Rusty took it from her. Then he bent down, picked up the chainsaw, and stood back up again. It wasn't comfortable to do so, but again, it was a relief to know that he could still bend down, pick up something, and stand back up again. He gave the chainsaw to Mia.

The wolves snarled.

Rusty and Mia were going to have to jump right into the fray, axe and chainsaw swinging. There was an excellent chance that this was going to be the demise of at least one of them. The way things had been going, it would probably be Rusty who didn't survive, so while it wasn't an ideal overall outcome, he'd prefer it to watching Mia die.

She tugged on the chainsaw cord. There was nothing left of Rusty's pride by now, so he wouldn't have given a shit if it had effortlessly roared to life. But it took her seven or eight tugs to get it going.

They gave each other a solemn look.

There was a lot to be said, but no time to say it.

They looked down at the creatures.

The moment had arrived.

They continued to stand there, waiting for a different moment.

Rusty was one hundred percent positive that the current moment was just as good as the prior one, but they continued to just stand there. They knew it had to be done, but it just seemed so fucking *stupid* to leave the porch when there were four wolves and a bobcat right there.

Mia, apparently having decided she could tough it out for a few more seconds at least, slashed at the wolf closest to her. Though there was chainsaw/fur contact, the blade only barely grazed the wolf's shoulder and caused no injury that Rusty could see.

There was a thunderous crash behind them as the side of the cabin collapsed.

This should not have been a positive development. It should have made Rusty and Mia even more screwed than they were before. But it frightened the wolves.

The wolves fled from the noise and the spewing flames.

Only the bobcat stayed where it was. Three swings of the chainsaw and two swings of the axe reduced its threat level.

Mia handed Rusty the chainsaw, then scooped up the two boards. One of them was on fire, but she swished it back and forth a few times and the flame went out. Rusty took his own burning strips of wood.

They hurried down the steps as the other side of the

cabin crashed to the ground.

JEFF STRAND

CHAPTER FOURTEEN

Though Rusty was overwhelmingly focused on survival and not property, it was still heartbreaking to see their home transform into a burning wreck. He'd had a pretty great life in that place. Even if they lived through this nightmare, it was entirely possible that his cherished, peaceful existence deep in the woods was over.

But that was a problem for later.

Rusty turned off the chainsaw and shoved it into the backpack. It slid right in, even though he couldn't see what he was doing behind him, and he vowed that there wouldn't be a repeat of the previous ineptitude.

The wolves were still staying away. This surely wasn't going to last.

A ball of flame scurried toward the woods. Rusty's best guess was that it was a squirrel that had been on top of the cabin when it collapsed. It didn't quite make it to the trees, instead stopping only about ten feet away from the cabin.

As Rusty and Mia began to walk down the driveway,

he let out a wince of pain.

"Are you going to be able to do this?" Mia asked.

Rusty nodded as he kept walking. "Yeah, yeah. That was a wince of embarrassment. You know, because my pants are so burnt up. I look ridiculous."

"Seriously, how bad does it hurt?"

"I'm not gonna lie. It does sting quite a bit." Rusty was lying. The pain was excruciating. The wood hadn't protected him as much as he thought.

"We can hide you somewhere. Build you a fort. I promise I'll come back for you."

"No. I'm going to slow us down and I apologize for that, but I can also swing an axe and a chainsaw just fine. If I feel like I'm going to get you killed, I swear I'll go hide somewhere, but for now I think we'll die if we split up."

"All right," said Mia. "Just making the offer."

"And I appreciate it." Yes, each step hurt, but it wasn't as if Rusty was hobbling around like a ninety-year-old. The wood was slowing him down more than the pain. He still deeply regretted that they hadn't done Mia first; sadly, the roll of duct tape would be a melted pile of silver goo by now.

No wolves had come for them. They'd scattered into the forest, and maybe they weren't coming back.

Rusty and Mia stepped off the dirt driveway into the thin forest in front of the cabin. The driveway wound around so much that it would be stupid not to take this shortcut. This did increase the odds of Rusty taking a bad step and falling, but the sun was shining and he could see where he was going and as long as he didn't get overconfident and stop paying attention, he'd be fine.

Just thinking *I'll be fine* made Rusty suspect that he'd

step into a hole hidden by some leaves, pitch forward, and have a leg bone explode through the skin.

They walked through the forest without speaking. Mia switched the two boards she was carrying from under her left arm to under her right arm. She was breathing heavily—from their prior exertion, not just from carrying a couple of boards—but Rusty knew he'd be the one to call for a rest break when it was time. Of course, if the boards became too cumbersome, they'd toss them aside and collect some sticks when they reached the truck.

"I'm going to ask one more time, and then I'll shut up," said Mia. "Because I'm serious, you look like you're dying."

"I promise you I'm not dying. If the pain becomes more than I can handle, you have my word that I will turn into a complete baby and refuse to go any further. For now, I'm fine. If I sit somewhere and hide, there's more of a chance that my burns will get dirty and infected."

"All right. I'm trusting you to say when."

"I will."

They continued walking. Rusty was confident that he'd make it. It was only three miles. No big deal. Three measly little miles. It could've been so much worse.

Okay, maybe not. If the truck had gotten stuck further from the cabin, they would've made much more of an effort to get it out of the mud. And then the truck would've been conveniently located right in front of the cabin when the zombie animals began to attack. At this very moment they'd be in town, insisting to the police that they weren't insane, instead of walking through the Forest of Doom on burnt-up legs. So it could've been so much better.

There was a steady breeze. Normally Rusty enjoyed cool breezes, but this breeze seemed purposely designed by a vengeful God to blow out his fires. When one stick went out, Rusty frantically tried to relight it with the other, but that one went out, too. They weren't going to run back to the cabin to get more fire, so they'd just have to do without.

Rusty noticed something crawling on Mia's shoulder. He swatted it off.

"What was that?" she asked.

"Spider."

"Zombie spider?"

"Dunno."

"Do you think it even matters?"

Rusty shrugged. "I guess they'd be more aggressive. Maybe they'd work with the flies instead of trying to eat them."

"So, yes, it does matter."

"I'm going to say that no, that wasn't a zombie spider. It wasn't even a very big spider. I just didn't think you'd want it crawling on your shoulder."

"And you were right."

"Cool."

"I don't have a bug phobia," said Mia, "but suddenly I do have an undead bug phobia. So I'd like us to change the subject, if that's okay."

"I'm more than happy to talk about something else, if you—"

"*Wolf.*"

Rusty glanced to the side. A wolf was running through the forest toward them. It was definitely one that had fled from the collapsing cabin, because thick strips of flesh were hanging off its side where Mia had blasted it with the shotgun. Rusty took a deep breath and braced himself. If he timed the swing properly and stepped out of the way at just the right moment, he might be able to incapacitate the wolf without even being knocked to the ground.

The wolf was only a few seconds away. He could do this.

Five...four...three...

The wolf leapt into the air, which quite honestly was something Rusty should have anticipated. He adjusted his swing.

The axe struck the wolf directly beneath its neck. The force of the collision knocked Rusty to the ground, and he let out a cry as he landed on something sharp. He lost his grip on the weapon.

Mia smacked the wolf with the boards. It flopped onto its side, the axe still imbedded in its body. It quickly began to get back to its feet.

Rusty grabbed the axe handle and wrenched it free.

Mia bashed the wolf directly on top of the head. One of the boards cracked.

Rusty slammed the axe into the side of the wolf's neck. He was still on the ground and not able to swing the axe very well, so it didn't go in deep. He pulled the blade free and did it again, with a bit more success.

Mia, apparently realizing that it would not do to break their boards, kicked the wolf in the side, hard enough to fracture one of its visible ribs.

The wolf's jaws snapped in the air, only inches away from taking a bite out of Mia's belly.

Rusty sat up and brought the axe blade down upon the wolf's neck. This time it sunk in deep. Not deep enough to sever its head, but deep enough that the next blow did the trick. The wolf's jaws clamped down upon Mia's foot. She screamed and kicked its head away.

The rest of the wolf's body ran at Rusty, missed him, and kept running until it struck a tree. It kept running and smacking into trees, almost as if it was inside a pinball machine. After the fifth or sixth hit, it dropped to the ground and lay there, twitching.

Rusty tried to stand up. Couldn't. He reached out and let Mia help him to his feet.

"Good kick," he said, with a slight wheeze.

"Thank you."

"I'm okay."

"You look bright and healthy. You're almost glowing."

"Has it been three miles yet?" Rusty asked.

"*Wolf.*"

"Aw, fuck me."

This one went a little better. Rusty still got knocked to the ground, but he didn't land on anything pointy, and Mia didn't have to risk breaking her boards. He was also able to get up by himself. He did have to slam the axe into the prone wolf over and over, like he was chopping wood, but by the time he was done it could only come after them if somebody carried it.

They resumed their walk. Both of them were too exhausted to resume their conversation.

A couple of minutes later, they emerged from the forest onto the road. They'd now follow it all the way to the truck. There were currently no zombie animals that they could see.

Okay, Rusty would normally walk a mile in about twenty minutes. So an hour to the truck under standard conditions. He wasn't walking *that* much slower than usual; his seared legs and the desperate need for haste mostly balanced each other out. An hour and ten minutes. Maybe an hour and fifteen. Plus however much time they spent battling the wilderness creatures.

They could make it. People had made it longer distances through more treacherous conditions, presumably.

"Do you think we should be quiet or loud?" Mia asked.

Rusty wasn't sure. Normally you'd be loud—bears and other dangerous animals would keep away if they heard you approaching. Was that true now? Would the sound of their voices attract danger?

"I'd say to just stick to normal speaking voices," said Rusty. "For now."

"Okay."

"And there's something I have to tell you."

"Is it bad?"

"Probably not."

"Your tone makes it sound really bad."

"I'm sure it's nothing," said Rusty. "It would just be irresponsible not to tell you. The squirrel bit me on the neck."

"The squirrel we put in the pot?"

Rusty shook his head. "The latest one."

"Oh."

"I don't feel weird. I don't feel dizzy. I can't even feel the bite anymore. But since we don't know exactly what we're dealing with, I couldn't keep that information from you."

"Let me see," said Mia. "Where is it?"

"On the back."

Mia let him move one step ahead of her. A moment later, she returned to her spot by his side. "It's not a very big bite."

"No."

"And it's not swollen or anything."

"That's good."

"It's not pulsating or leaking."

"Enough."

"I'm glad you told me. We'll keep an eye on it. Right now it doesn't look like it's anything to worry about. As soon as we get to town we'll drench it in antiseptic and get you to a doctor. I mean, we'd get you to a doctor anyway because of your legs, but we'll disinfect it before we get there."

"Yeah," said Rusty, who was briefly troubled by the thought of hospitals packed to capacity, turning away patients, infected people on gurneys filling the hallways.

He shook away the thought. He'd worry about that if they emerged into a zombie-plagued hellscape. For now, they just needed to focus on the simple, straightforward task of getting to the truck.

The flames from the cabin were no longer visible behind them, though the smoke still billowed into the air. On a day with fewer problems, Rusty would worry that the burning cabin would start a forest fire. Though for all he knew, the government might have to burn the whole thing down anyway, and he was giving them a head start.

Stop it, he told himself. The scope of this plague, or curse, or whatever was unknown. No need to stress out over a worst-case scenario. He should be thinking happy thoughts, like about how there weren't thousands of undead animals pouring out of the woods onto the dirt road. He and Mia could easily be skeletonized right now. A few minutes into their journey, things were proceeding relatively smoothly.

"Do you hear something?" Mia asked.

Rusty listened carefully but didn't stop moving. "Like what?"

"A knocking."

"From where?"

Mia gestured with the boards. "Those trees over there. Probably a woodpecker."

Now Rusty did hear it. *Tap, tap, tap.* She was right: probably a woodpecker. He could narrow the source of the sound to a couple of large trees, but he couldn't see the actual bird. "Yeah, that's probably what it is."

"Zombie woodpecker?"

"I hope not."

"That would be a humiliating way to die."

"Not as bad as being killed by a zombie squirrel," said Rusty.

"We need another pact. If one of us gets killed by a zombie woodpecker, we tell people that they were killed by something else, like a zombie rhinoceros."

"I don't think the coroner would buy it."

"We don't have to lie to the coroner. I just mean the general public. I don't want my legacy to be death by zombie woodpecker. I don't want people to pretend that it was a horrible tragedy but not be able to control their snickering."

"Or doing a Woody Woodpecker laugh."

"What's that?"

Rusty didn't think he could accurately mimic a Woody Woodpecker laugh. "I'll play it for you when we get to town. He's a cartoon character."

"Do the laugh."

"No."

"Do it. We have time. Entertain me. Take my mind off

my troubles."

"No."

"You shouldn't have brought it up if you weren't willing to do the laugh."

"Oh, hey, we were right," said Rusty, pointing at the red bird that came into view from the back of one of the trees.

The woodpecker tapped on the tree a few more times, then flew off the branch.

Rusty realized that it was flying toward them.

Dive-bombing them.

In about two seconds, the idea of being murdered by a woodpecker went from amusing conversation fodder to almost bladder-releasing terror.

"Watch out!" Rusty said.

He was pretty good with the axe, but he wasn't confident that he was "whack a bird in mid-air" good with it. Their best bet was to go defensive; crouch down, drop their weapons, and cover their faces.

Rusty dropped to his knees, which hurt like hell. Mia did the same thing. He covered his face with both hands. There was a *swish* as the bird sailed right past them.

He removed his hands and glanced to the side. The bird flew in an arc, like a boomerang, and came back toward them again.

This time it came so close to the back of Rusty's neck that he could feel the breeze as it shot past him. He looked over and saw it turning around once more. On its third pass, it came so close that a feather brushed against his skin.

Was this fucking bird trying to mess with them?

He still didn't think he could get it with the axe, but the planks had a lot more surface area, and if he and Mia

166

both took a swing maybe they could knock Woody out of the air. He told Mia his plan, speaking very quickly because the bird was making its fourth swoop at them.

She handed him one of the boards. They stood up.

They moved far enough from each other that their boards wouldn't collide (and that one of them wouldn't accidentally knock the other unconscious), then prepared themselves for the bird's next attack. At least it was only one bird. For now. There were a lot of frickin' birds in the forest.

The bird flew at them.

Rusty and Mia both swung and missed.

This was really bad. Rusty wasn't filled with unimaginable horror at the thought of a zombie woodpecker, but they were wasting a lot of time. They couldn't afford to be standing around swinging boards at a bird. Who knew what other dangers were moving through the forest toward them?

The bird, clearly not tired of the game, swooped at them yet again.

Rusty swung and missed, and then the woodpecker landed in his hair.

It wasted no time in slamming its beak against the top of his head. He cried out; it felt like somebody hammering a nail into his skull. The woodpecker jabbed him three more times before he could frantically brush it off.

The bird flew into the air, circled them a few times, then attacked Rusty again. This time it only got in one peck before he brushed it away. He lunged at it, trying to snatch the bird out of the air so he could squash it in his hands, but didn't come close.

He could feel a trickle of blood running down his

forehead. Mia's eyes widened at the sight of it.

"Don't worry," he told her. "Head wounds bleed a lot."

At least it hadn't pierced his skull, to the best of his knowledge.

Mia swung at the woodpecker and came so close that a tail feather drifted to the ground.

The bird landed on Rusty's shoulder and pecked at his neck, three times in rapid succession, not far from where the squirrel had bit him. He tried unsuccessfully to grab it again. Its beak hadn't gone deep, but it had definitely broken the skin.

Now he sort of agreed with Mia: having fended off grizzly bears, wolves, and bobcats, he did not want to be murdered by a woodpecker. Its beak really hurt, and he didn't want people to giggle about his demise.

The bird flew off his shoulder. Rusty and Mia both swung at it at the same time, their boards smacking into each other so hard that Rusty dropped his. This was really becoming ridiculous.

The woodpecker flew straight at Mia's face.

She put up her hand to protect herself. It pecked at her palm. Mia squeezed her hand into a fist, trying to grab the rotten fucking bastard's neck, but wasn't able to catch it.

It flew at her face again.

Its beak plunged deep into her left eye.

CHAPTER FIFTEEN

Mia shrieked.

She grabbed the bird, broke its neck, and flung its dead body to the ground. She continued shrieking as she stomped on it, over and over, her left hand pressed tightly over her eye.

"Let me see it," Rusty said, trying to pretend that he was calm.

Mia wouldn't move her hand.

"Mia, please, I need to see how bad it is."

She continued to stomp on the flattened, bloodless bird. Rusty placed his hands on her shoulders. She stepped away from him. *"Just leave me alone!"*

He'd give her ten seconds to stop freaking out. They simply could not afford to lose any time due to this injury. It was suddenly even *more* important that they get to the truck as soon as possible. In her situation, he'd stand there screaming, too, but he had to be an unsympathetic asshole or they were both dead.

But she could have the ten seconds. *Ten...nine...eight...*

Mia fell to her knees. Rusty tried another comforting

hand on her shoulder and she shook it off. Her whole body trembled as she sobbed.

Rusty's heart raced and his stomach churned. He glanced around to see if any predators had emerged from the woods. For the moment, they were okay. That wouldn't last many more moments.

Before the ten seconds was over, Mia stood back up. She was still crying and she still had her hand pressed tightly over her eye, but she'd regained a bit of her composure. Rusty gently placed his hand on hers, and she didn't resist when he moved it away.

Her left eye was closed. However, any magical fantasy that Rusty had simply *imagined* the bird slamming its sharp beak into the orb was erased by the amount of blood around her eye and on her palm.

"Can you open it?" Rusty asked.

Mia shook her head.

"We need to see how bad..."

Rusty trailed off. Why did he need to see how bad it was? What was he going to do, make a medical diagnosis and come up with a treatment plan? He knew how bad it was: really fucking horrifically bad. He didn't need to gaze upon that grisly sight to acquire further information.

"It's going to be okay," he told her. "Just keep it closed. We'll be at the truck in an hour, and we'll be in town right after that, and we'll get you fixed up."

"They're going to have to cut out my eye."

"You're not a doctor and I'm not a doctor, so we don't know that."

"Don't bullshit me, Uncle Rusty."

"You might lose the eye. You might not. We don't know what kind of surgery they can do when something like this happens." That was the truth. However, the trickle of blood actively leaking from between her eyelids made it clear that, yes, the doctors would almost certainly have to remove her eye. But why not give her some hope? They had plenty of harsh reality to deal with right now. "They've got lasers and stuff. I'm not *promising* you that they can fix it; I'm just saying that they *might* be able to fix it."

"Okay."

"How bad does it hurt?"

"More than I can even describe."

"Keep your hand away from it. Other than that, we'll just fight through this."

"Oh, shit, I shouldn't have put my hand over it," said Mia. "It's going to get infected!"

"We can't worry about that right now. And you didn't actually touch it, right? You just covered it."

"Right."

"So you're fine. Keep your hand away from it. We're in a race against time, but not because of possible infection. We'll get it cleaned out long before that's an issue. You're being very brave, Mia."

"I appreciate that, but I'm not six."

"Sorry. I think you were just trying to upstage my burnt legs."

"Let's not talk unless we need to." Mia sniffled and wiped her nose on her sleeve. "Can you hand me the boards?"

"Do you still want to carry them?"

"It didn't peck off my fingers."

Rusty picked up the boards and gave them to her. Though he felt positively sick to his stomach, he forced himself not to vomit. It would've been from the stress, but he didn't want Mia to think he'd puked because of her eye.

"You're bleeding pretty bad," Mia informed him.

Rusty blinked and realized that blood was running down his own face. He wiped it away. "It looks worse than it is."

"Does it hurt?"

"Not as bad as my legs and not as bad as your eye. My head is a low priority." He picked up the axe. "Let's get moving."

It was difficult to have an optimistic mindset right now. Still, he couldn't deny that while his niece was being stabbed in the eye by a woodpecker, no other attacks had happened. The idea of this being a leisurely stroll down a scenic path was outside of the realm of possibility, but it also might not be a constant battle for survival.

They resumed their walk. Mia sniffled frequently, and red tears trickled down her left cheek, but she was no longer in a panic. Rusty didn't speak to her. He was awful at offering comforting words and decided to respect her "let's not talk unless we need to" request.

He cringed as another bird flew overhead. He and Mia continued walking, watching it carefully. The bird continued on its way. Whether it was a normal bird, or an undead bird that simply hadn't seen the easy prey beneath it, they didn't know.

Up ahead, something rustled in the bushes.

It was not something small.

Rusty and Mia continued to walk. Maybe whatever it was would stay in the forest.

The bushes rustled again. They were too thick to get a clear look at what was moving through them, but Rusty was ninety-nine percent sure it was another bear. The one percent of uncertainty was due to the possibility that the holes in his head from the woodpecker were causing him to hallucinate.

Yes, he'd killed two bears today. Both of them were stuck at the time. Slaying a bear that was wedged in a window frame was a significantly different task than doing battle with a bear on its own terms.

Maybe they'd get lucky and the hallucination theory was correct.

About a hundred feet ahead of them, a grizzly bear emerged from the forest. It was smaller than the first bear, but bigger than the second one.

Maybe it wasn't an undead bear. Maybe it was just a regular old normal standard bear. In which case, it would realize its mistake and quickly go back the way it came.

Rusty couldn't see if it had bloodshot eyes, and there were no visible bones, at least not that he could see from his current vantage point. That said, the bear was walking right toward them, successfully conveying great menace.

"Go away!" Rusty shouted.

The bear did not go away.

Rusty tried to keep his fear hidden. He could deal with this situation in a rational manner. Yes, a giant grizzly bear was lumbering toward them, and there were no cabin walls to protect them, and he could no longer trust Mia to accurately aim a firearm, and he hadn't fought the previous two bears with blister-covered legs that hurt to move, but...

There was no "but." Those were all simply facts.

Mia dropped the boards onto the ground again. "I'll take the axe back," she said, reaching for it. Her trembling voice belied the badass tone of her words.

Rusty gave her the axe and took out the chainsaw.

The bear was not running toward them, which was

good, but nor was it pausing to reflect upon the proper course of action. Its mindset seemed to be: *I'm going to devour these two humans, who pose no danger to me, and because they cannot escape, there's no reason to rush and overly exert myself.*

"Are you sure we shouldn't run?" Mia asked.

"I don't think we'd be successful. And you know the rule for outrunning a bear."

"What's that?"

"You don't have to outrun the bear. You just have to outrun me."

Mia nodded as though she got the joke, though she didn't smile. "I love you too much for that."

"By the way, if it *does* take me down, run. If killing me distracts the bear and you squander the opportunity to get away, I'll haunt you, big-time. Steal my chainsaw and go. Got it?"

"Not gonna leave you to die, but I appreciate the offer."

Rusty didn't like that answer, but he needed to cut this conversation short. He pulled the cord of the chainsaw, praying it would start.

It almost started. Not quite.

He tugged on the cord again, pulling so hard that it felt like he practically wrenched his arm out of its socket. The chainsaw roared to life. But the pain in his arm didn't immediately fade, because that's exactly what he needed right now: another part of his body that hurt.

The bear, not intimidated, continued to walk toward them.

Mia raised the axe. She was going to be swinging a heavy bladed weapon around without the benefit of depth perception, but Rusty was sure nothing bad would happen with that.

Rusty raised the chainsaw. They hadn't discussed whether they should run toward the bear, or just wait for it to reach them. Rusty decided to wait. If they charged at the bear, it might do the same to them, and he preferred a scenario where the bear just calmly strolled right into the whirring chainsaw.

It was only about twenty feet away. It looked very, very, very large. Bears seemed quite a bit bigger when they weren't stuck in a window frame.

He and Mia were dead. Humans didn't defeat bears in up-close combat. It just didn't happen. They should have fled and taken their chances climbing up a tree, even though there was no way in hell Rusty could scale a tree in his current condition. This was insane. This was suicide.

The bear kept walking toward them. It was looking directly at Rusty with its bloodshot eyes. It didn't roar, but it showed off its teeth in what Rusty swore was a sadistic grin.

Rusty waved the chainsaw around in the air, hoping that the bear would get the hint that he was wielding a dangerous weapon. Mia swung her axe around to send the same message. Several streaks of blood ran all the way down her left cheek, and she actually looked pretty frightening, but the bear did not slow its gait.

What should he aim for? Its head? Chest? One of its front legs? Slicing off one of its legs could conceivably cause it to fall over and not be able to get back up, after which they could casually stroll off into the distance.

Rusty's arms were shaking badly and his palms were so drenched in sweat that he could barely sustain his grip on the chainsaw. The way things were going, he figured there was a fifty-fifty chance that he'd drop the weapon and slice off his own foot instead of the bear's.

With only about five feet separating them, the bear stopped moving.

It stood up to its full height, which was extremely tall, raised its arms in the air, and let out a roar. Could Rusty hear it over the chainsaw? No. Was it still positively terrifying? Yes. He wanted to run away screaming, and he also wanted to drop into the fetal position and just hope for the best. Instead, he stood his ground.

The bear dropped back to all fours. It roared, giving Rusty and Mia a blast of its hot breath. Rusty had no basis for comparison on how a bear's breath should smell, but had the reek of something that was rotting inside. Then it resumed walking toward them.

Rusty tensed up, ready to slash at its shoulder. Could he saw through its entire front leg before the bear tore a twelve-pound chunk of flesh out of Rusty's body? He was about to find out...

The bear stood up again, as if trying to accentuate their size difference even more clearly now that it was a couple of feet closer. It seemed like overkill, though Rusty had to admit that he did receive the message.

He lunged forward with the chainsaw.

The bear swiveled. Not enough to make Rusty miss completely, but enough that he thrust the chainsaw blade into the center of its chest instead of its shoulder. The blade sunk in deep, completely disappearing into the bear, going all the way to the chainsaw's hand guard. Then the weapon popped out of Rusty's grasp.

Rusty hurriedly stepped back as the bear took a vicious swipe at him. He couldn't feel the air swish in front of him but he certainly got a good look at the bear's claws. If they'd hit their target, his entire face would've landed on the ground with a splat.

The chainsaw remained embedded in the bear's chest, slowly working its way down like a zipper.

The bear backhanded him with the same paw that had just missed. Rusty stumbled backwards, dazed, then fell to the ground. He put a hand to his face—it was still intact.

Guts spilled from the bear's belly. It dropped to all fours, but the chainsaw didn't fall out. The blade must've been wedged against a rib or something.

Rusty tried to stand up but couldn't get his legs to move properly.

Mia slammed the axe into the bear's shoulder. She wrenched it out and struck it again. Then, in a move that Rusty could not believe he was actually seeing performed by his niece, she grabbed a thick handful of fur with her left hand, slammed the axe blade deep into the bear's back to give her leverage with her right, and pulled herself up onto its back like she was mounting a very large, hairy, psychotic horse.

Rusty blinked. He couldn't have really seen that. Clearly the bear had knocked his brain out of whack.

No...Mia was indeed on the bear's back, like she'd transformed into a nimble elf in a fantasy novel.

Rusty's inclination was to just lay on the ground and gape at the sight before him, but he should probably try to help her, or at least put himself in a spot where he wouldn't get trampled.

Mia whacked the axe blade into the bear's back, over and over and over.

When the bear stood up, she kept a tight grip on it with her left hand and tried to get in another chop of the axe, but that was too much even during this jaw-dropping display of agility, and she fell to the ground.

The chainsaw still hadn't fallen out of the bear, though many of its internal organs had.

Rusty shakily got to his feet while he removed the rifle strap from over his shoulder. Without Mia in the way, he could open fire. It wouldn't do much good without incredible precision, but he might luck out and blind the beast.

Mia scooted away from the bear. She still held the axe.

Rusty fired several times in rapid succession. Pieces of the bear's head came off, but none of the shots hit either of its eyes. All this did was make it slightly angrier than it had already been, and the bear dropped to all fours and gave Rusty its full attention.

He fired a couple more times. The first shot struck the bear right above its eye, and the second shot struck the bear right below its eye, a feat he could not have accomplished on purpose even if the bear was a stationary target. If he kept this up, its eyeball might just roll out of its head.

His next two shots also missed the bear's eyes. The last one missed its head altogether. He squeezed the trigger again—nothing, the rifle was out of ammunition. There was more in his backpack, but since the bear was walking toward him in an extremely menacing manner he didn't think there'd be time to dig it out and reload the gun.

Mia slammed the axe into the bear's head. Clearly the adrenaline was flowing, because the axe went in deep.

Got it in the eye.

The bear jerked its head away, taking the axe with it. Now both of their most useful weapons were embedded in the bear.

Mia's axe hit was cause for celebration, but there was a

big difference between a one-eyed bear and a zero-eyed bear. The situation was still dire. Rusty wondered if Mia and the bear might bond over their shared optical trauma.

The chainsaw dropped out of the bear's belly.

However, the weapon was not currently accessible, considering that it was underneath an angry zombie grizzly bear. Rusty spun the rifle around in his hands, in case he needed to use it to bash the bear across the face.

The bear swatted at the axe handle but couldn't get it free. Rusty frantically scooted backwards, right to the edge of the dirt road. The bear followed. The axe in its face should have made it look less threatening, but it actually made it look even scarier.

Though Rusty wasn't very happy that the bear was coming toward him, it *did* mean that Mia was able to snatch up the chainsaw. She hoisted it above her head like Leatherface, ran into the right position, and slammed the blade into the bear's face, chewing up its remaining eye.

The bear shifted directions, roaring in fury.

It still had their axe. They needed their axe.

Rusty tossed the rifle aside and forced himself to stand up. He was grateful that his grunts of pain were drowned out by the sound of the chainsaw. He and Mia both tried to grab the axe handle while avoiding contact with the thrashing bear, which seemed like it should be easier than everything else they'd done the past couple of minutes yet turned out to be a nightmare. Mia shut off the chainsaw, presumably so that the bear wouldn't go after the sound, but the bear just wouldn't stop moving.

The axe handle smashed into Rusty's hand so hard that he thought he might have broken some fingers.

Finally, Mia (of course) got a hold of the handle and pulled it out of the bear's skull. Rusty and Mia hurriedly moved away from the creature, which walked off the road and bashed into a tree. The sight was not as comedic as it should have been.

They both stood there, exhausted and gasping for breath. But as long as they didn't stupidly stumble right into the bear's path, it was no longer going to pose a problem for them.

Mia wiped some blood from her face. "I don't think we're going to make it to the truck."

"Of course we are," said Rusty. "We just defeated another fuckin' bear!"

"I can't keep doing this."

"If we can beat a bear, we can beat anything. We can do this, Mia."

"I got my *eye* poked out, Uncle Rusty. I just want to go to sleep."

"No, no, no, it's going to be fine," said Rusty, who knew this wasn't the time to be a pedantic asshole who pointed out that her eye got stabbed but not poked out. "Bears are the biggest things out here. If we can fight them, we can fight anything. We're in good shape. We're..."

Rusty trailed off. Yes, they'd done battle with the largest animal out here, but there was another pack of wolves emerging from the forest. Three...four...five...six...oh, yeah, they were in bad shape.

Mia gave Rusty the chainsaw. It didn't fall right out of his hand, so he assumed that his fingers weren't actually broken.

He pulled on the starter cord a few times. It didn't even sputter. Three more wolves joined the others.

"Okay, I lied," Rusty admitted. "We're not in good shape."

JEFF STRAND

CHAPTER SIXTEEN

Rusty couldn't deny that he sort of agreed with Mia. The idea of lying on the comfy ground, going to sleep, and not worrying about how things turned out did have some appeal.

No. No, it didn't.

They were going to survive this, even though they didn't have a working chainsaw or a burning cabin to protect them from the wolves. They might be up against an entire forest of zombie animals, but he and Mia were humans, and humans kicked ass. Yes, it would help if the wolves approached them slowly, one at a time, and perhaps lowered their heads to make it convenient for Mia to slam her axe into their necks. Wolves were known for being considerate, right? Everything was going to turn out just fine.

Mia dropped her axe.

"Don't give up," Rusty told her.

"I didn't," she said. "There was blood on my hand and it slipped." She bent down and retrieved the axe.

All of the wolves began to growl.

"You take the four on the left," said Rusty. "I'll take the five on the right."

"Uh-huh."

"Unless you want five and I'll take four."

"I can't tell if you're joking or not."

"I don't know if I'm joking or not," Rusty admitted.

He suspected that it was less "joking" than "complete self-delusion." They couldn't fight nine wolves. It simply wasn't going to happen. One wolf each? Maybe. *Maybe*. But the only way they were going to win a battle against nine wolves was if the wolves were from outer space and it was suddenly revealed that they weren't immune to the common cold. That was it—extreme susceptibility to human germs was their only hope. And the fact that these animals already seemed to be rotting on the inside implied that bacteria was not going to be their downfall.

Rusty felt surprisingly calm considering that he was likely to be dead a minute from now. Perhaps he was getting used to the sensation of impending doom. He tugged on the chainsaw cord and nothing happened. Hopefully he could at least bonk one of the wolves on the head with it before they shredded him.

Some bushes rustled behind them.

Rusty and Mia glanced back over their shoulders as a deer stepped out of the woods.

Wonderful. Zombie deer. Was that more or less humiliating than death by zombie squirrel? Squirrels were much smaller, but deer were known for their passive, gentle nature. After a split-second of thought, Rusty decided that the deer killing him would be preferable to a squirrel doing it, so he had that ray of sunshine left.

The deer looked fine, though. Healthy. Rusty couldn't see its eyes, but this particular deer might not be part of the cursed army of the undead.

The deer turned and ran.

The wolves charged.

Mia raised the axe as if she might be able to decapitate all nine of them with one swing.

"Don't do anything," Rusty told her.

Though making the choice not to defend themselves was risky, Rusty had an odd feeling about the way the wolves were running. They were veering to the side of the road, all nine of them, as if their chosen prey was the deer and not the humans. It was a pretty narrow road and Rusty couldn't be certain of his theory, but "stand there calmly and hope not to be noticed" seemed to be their best bet at living through this.

He started to doubt himself as the wolves got closer.

But it didn't matter. Trying to fight off nine wolves with an axe and a non-working chainsaw would have the exact same result as just standing there. Might as well test his theory and hope for the best.

The wolves ran past them into the forest.

Rusty couldn't believe it. He supposed that they preferred succulent venison to stringy human flesh. He hoped that the deer would escape after taking them on a nice long run far from here, and that it wouldn't end up like the massacred deer they'd found by the creek ages ago, back when he thought things in the forest were merely a bit quaint. That deer hadn't been eaten, so the "succulent" theory probably wasn't right, but it didn't matter. The wolves had selected a different target.

They were saved. All they needed was for a deer to conveniently show up whenever a pack of wolves was nearby, and they could just stroll right to the truck with nary a care in the world.

"Let's get moving," Rusty told Mia, even though she'd started moving the moment the last wolf sped past them.

More goddamn rustling behind them.

One of the wolves ran back onto the road, as if deciding that there wasn't going to be much deer meat left after the others were finished tearing it apart. It rushed straight at Mia, who slammed the axe into its head just as the wolf bashed into her, knocking her to the ground.

Rusty dropped the chainsaw and kicked the wolf in the head as hard as he could. There was a loud *snap*, presumably from its neck breaking. It continued to try to bite Mia, but its lopsided head was making that difficult. Rusty snatched the axe from Mia, then chopped at the back of the wolf's head, over and over, striking it with as much power and speed as possible while staying aware that his niece was directly underneath it and that missing the wolf could have disastrous consequences.

Mia scooted out from underneath the wolf as Rusty got in the last hit. Its head fell to the ground. The wolf rolled onto its back and frantically clawed at the air with all four legs.

Rusty returned the axe to Mia and picked up his chainsaw. Mia gathered the two boards and they resumed the process of getting the hell out of there.

"Are you okay?" Rusty asked.

"I'm missing an eye."

"I mean, did the wolf hurt you more than you were already hurt?"

Mia shrugged. "Scratched the shit out of me. But it didn't touch my other eye."

They picked up the pace. Every stride had hurt before, but kicking the wolf in the head had done Rusty no favors in that regard. Still, with Mia slowly bleeding from the eyeball, Rusty made a strong effort not to grunt in pain with every step. Things were much worse for her.

They walked without speaking for a few minutes, the only sound coming from their footsteps and heavy breathing. A few minutes without an animal attack. This was nice.

Mia wiped more blood from her face. Rusty wished they had something to cover her wound, but he didn't want to tear off a strip of his germ-laden clothing. Anything they had available to put over her eye would almost certainly lead to infection, and Rusty couldn't imagine anything worse than a swollen, infected, pus-filled eye socket.

It was going to be awful when they finally put antiseptic on it. When he held her hand during the process, he'd be prepared for her to crush every bone in it.

They walked for a few more minutes. The pain was bothering him quite a bit less now that Rusty's legs were almost completely numb. He wasn't wearing a watch, but he estimated that they'd been walking about ten minutes without a vicious attempt on their lives. They hadn't gone a mile yet, but they were making good time for a couple of exhausted and injured people. What if they were walking away from danger instead of toward it? He and Mia might have escaped and simply didn't realize it yet.

As they went around the next curve, Rusty frowned.

"What's that?" Mia asked.

"I'm not sure."

Up ahead, the road was covered with small animals. Lots of them. They filled the entire path. They seemed too small to be problematic, although considering the amount of trouble they'd had with a single squirrel and a single woodpecker, Rusty wasn't going to get overly confident quite yet.

They kept walking. A few steps later it became clear what they were dealing with.

"Oh, fuck," said Mia.

Porcupines. Zombie porcupines.

It wasn't like a *wall* of porcupines. They were spaced out enough that, conceivably, it was possible to quickly and carefully make their way past them. But one quill jabbed deep into their ankle would pretty much be the end of their journey and thus their lives. And Rusty had no trouble envisioning a scenario in which a porcupine brushed against him, causing him to fall forward and land on several more. It wasn't as if the other fates that had potentially awaited him were pleasant, but death by hundreds of porcupine quills seemed like a particularly horrific way to go.

Mia shoved the axe into her backpack. "Put away the chainsaw," she told Rusty. "We'll just clear a path with the boards."

"What if they swarm us?"

"Do you have a better idea?"

"Go around them. Go through the woods for a bit."

"We can't see what's on the ground in the woods. I'd feel safer just knocking porcupines out of the way."

Rusty wasn't sure he agreed with that, but he was willing to acquiesce to the person with one eye. He put the chainsaw in the backpack—it would be nice to not have to carry it around, but it might start again and he didn't want to leave it behind—and took a board from Mia. He considered starting a conversation about possible nicknames for zombie porcupines to distract them from the possibility of agonizing stinging pain, but decided against it.

They walked at a normal pace. The porcupines, at least a hundred of them, were moving toward them. Rusty knew very little about the species, but he was almost positive that porcupines lived in much smaller groups, and he'd definitely never heard of a whole wave of them moving forward like this. Even in his self-imposed isolation, a deadly porcupine caravan seemed like an anecdote he would've heard.

They'd almost reached each other. Rusty was ready with the board. Time for these zombupines to learn that you didn't mess with humans who were carrying large pieces of wood.

He smacked the closest one out of the way. It didn't roll as far as he would've hoped. Mia smacked one and got a little more distance.

Rusty was almost positive that the things he'd heard about porcupines being able to shoot their quills at predators was incorrect. Almost.

The first porcupine hurried toward him, presumably very angry about being struck with the board. In fact, all of the porcupines seemed to be more pissed off now than they had been before Rusty and Mia went on the offensive.

Mia picked up her pace, swinging the board back and forth, hitting a porcupine each time. Rusty tried the same tactic. This was doing a decent job of clearing a path in front of them, but none of the porcupines they hit were calling it quits, so they had spiky creatures coming at them from all directions.

Rusty smacked one really, really hard, actually getting some aerial distance. He felt no pride or sense of accomplishment for this.

The porcupines were swarming them.

The boards taped to Rusty's legs would provide some protection, but they were meant to keep out teeth and claws. There was plenty of room for a very thin quill to penetrate.

They were still making forward progress; just not anywhere near as quickly as they'd like. Right now they were directly in the center of the mass of porcupines, but as long as there wasn't a disaster…

Rusty noticed that one of them was right behind Mia's foot.

He wasn't able to get the entirety of "Watch out!" shouted before the porcupine ran into her. Mia cried out and stumbled forward, which caused her to step on a different porcupine. She dropped the board and her arms flailed as she desperately struggled to keep her balance.

She toppled forward.

Rusty lunged toward her, hoping to break her fall. He missed.

Mia dropped to the porcupine-covered ground.

Her landing was not exactly an Olympic-level feat of dexterity. But it was impressive nevertheless, because the board had landed on a couple of porcupines, and her hands landed on the board, leaving her in kind of a yoga position and sparing her the experience of having dozens of quills stabbing into her belly.

Rusty grabbed her by the back of the pants and pulled her back up.

He smacked the closest porcupines away from her, giving her the chance to retrieve her board. The two porcupines that had been under the board were twitching but not walking around, especially the one whose guts were on the outside. Rusty and Mia went back to trying to clear themselves a path forward.

A quill protruded from the back of Mia's foot. It was just going to have to stay there until the road cleared up enough for her to get a chance to reach down and pluck it out.

Rusty noticed that Mia was smacking the porcupines with more hostility than she'd been showing before. He didn't blame her. Rusty kept knocking the little shits out of his way. There were now several quills imbedded in his board, so hopefully those were doing an extra bit of damage.

His arms had already been aching. Now they felt like they were going to pop free with each swing of the board. At least they kept moving forward, so it wouldn't be much longer before...

He cursed for the several hundredth time that day. Yes, they were moving forward, but the mass of porcupines was moving along with them. They weren't making any progress toward escaping them. The truck was still far away; they couldn't just keep smacking porcupines the entire way there. Rusty would be lucky to keep it going all the way to the curve up ahead.

"We'll have to run," he told Mia.

"You can't run."

"I'll find a hidden reserve of strength somewhere. What we're doing now isn't working."

"What if you fall?"

"I probably will. And then I'll die a horrible fucking death. But that's how this is going to play out anyway, so we might as well go for it."

Mia nodded, causing a couple flecks of blood to come off her eye. "Count of three?"

"No, you go first."

"You're not sacrificing yourself, are you?"

"No, I'm not," Rusty said. "I might get to that point later but I'm not there yet. I just want to see how fast they follow you and see if it's even possible for me to outrun them."

"You'd better not be sacrificing yourself."

"I swear I'm not."

"All right. I'm trusting you."

Mia hurried forward. She wasn't able to break into a full run, but she vigorously swung the board back and forth and moved much faster than they'd been going. Faster than the porcupines. If she didn't step in the wrong spot, she was going to make it.

Rusty realized that he was paying more attention to his niece than his own predicament, and he knocked a few porcupines out of the way, adding to the collection of quills lodged in his board. If God was a porcupine, Rusty was going to have a lot to answer for in the afterlife.

The quill remained stuck in Mia's foot, but it didn't seem to be affecting her stride. Soon there were only a couple of porcupines near her, and she was able to knock both of them away.

That didn't look so hard.

Rusty could do this.

It would be fine.

It would be easy.

It might be slightly uncomfortable for a few moments, but nothing a guy like him couldn't handle. He wouldn't fall over. Not a chance. This was going to be very, very easy.

"C'mon!" said Mia.

Rusty moved, imagining himself a professional hockey

player knocking other players out of the way on the way to the winning goal. This mental image lasted about a second before being replaced by thoughts of him as an exhausted middle-aged man with burnt legs. The pain was staggering. He swung the board as quickly as he could, praying that he wouldn't trip or simply pass out from the agony.

He accidentally stepped on a porcupine's leg, somehow not getting jabbed by any quills in the process. He kicked the animal out of the way.

Rusty was getting past the worst of them.

It was looking as if he might get out of this without falling and dying by being stabbed by a thousand quills.

He wasn't wobbling. He wasn't even losing his balance.

Yes, his legs felt like they'd been set on fire again, but he was going to make it out of this particular mess without a disaster.

Almost there.

A porcupine's head practically exploded as he smashed the end of the board into it.

And then...

...he made it. All of the porcupines were behind him. If they kept up this pace for just a short while longer, they'd leave those spiny bastards in the dust.

"Good work, Uncle Rusty," said Mia. She grinned at him. He would never tell her that the grin, accented by blood that had trickled all the way down her face, was extremely creepy.

They kept moving. Yes, every step felt like a sadistic interrogator was taking a blowtorch to his skin, but pain was temporary. (Unless the pain from the burns was, in fact, quite permanent. He wouldn't worry about that now.) As long as his legs didn't break off at the knees, things were looking good for escaping this situation—by which he meant only the undead porcupines. He had no idea what other crap awaited them.

Before too long, they'd gone around a curve and the porcupines were no longer visible nor likely to catch up to them. Mia plucked the quill out of her foot, then resumed walking. Rusty decided to leave the quills in his board, which kind of made him feel like a badass.

"That wasn't so bad," Rusty noted.

"Certainly could've gone worse. They didn't poke out my other eye."

"Nope. They sure didn't."

"Could've happened."

"Yep."

"I think it's going to be easy from now on," said Mia. "I think we're just going to stroll on over to the truck. I bet we won't even need the boards—we'll just start the engine and it'll back right out of the mud. Then we'll drive into town, get my bionic eye installed, and have a nice lunch." She sounded like she was on the verge of a hysterical cackle while she spoke, but Rusty was impressed by her ability to keep it together after all they'd been through.

"Yeah. It's all fine from now on," said Rusty.

It took about three minutes for his comment to be proven as a lie—long enough that it didn't count as a goofy moment of irony. The pack of wolves, having presumably finished tearing the poor deer to shreds, was back for more prey.

Rusty and Mia dropped the boards and ran.

They had no expectations that they could outrun a pack of wolves. Instead, they ran off the road, heading for the nearest large tree. Rusty was amazed by what a sudden surge of adrenaline could do; he couldn't even feel his legs. Minutes ago he could barely move his arms, but they sure as hell worked *now*, as he and Mia frantically climbed up the same tree.

A wolf's jaws bit down upon his leg, hitting wood instead of flesh. They climbed a few more feet, getting themselves out of reach as long as these wolves didn't suddenly acquire the ability to scale trees, which didn't seem one hundred percent out of the question.

Eight wolves. The one whose neck Rusty had broken earlier wasn't with them. They walked around the tree, snarling.

"So," said Mia, "I guess we get to starve to death."

"We'd die of dehydration first."

"We've got bottled water."

"Not enough to outlast dying of starvation."

"So, I guess we get to die of dehydration."

Rusty didn't want to succumb to nihilism, but that did sound reasonable.

He hoped Mia didn't notice that there were birds circling above them.

CHAPTER SEVENTEEN

Mia did indeed notice the birds circling overhead. She cringed and placed a hand over her injured eye.

"It'll be okay," Rusty assured her.

The branches they were on seemed pretty sturdy, so they didn't have to worry about them snapping and sending them plunging down into the eight slavering wolf mouths below. Aside from the whole food and water situation, and the knowledge that no help was on its way, they could stay here in relative comfort for quite some time.

Mia removed her hand from her face and brushed something off her leg.

"What?" Rusty asked.

"Ants."

Yep. There were ants on his branch, too. He brushed off as many as he could, doing it quickly in an effort not to get stung. They spent a couple of productive minutes getting rid of the insects, sending many of them hurtling to their deaths. Just out of curiosity, Rusty squished one's head underneath his thumb. The rest of the ant did not continue to move. That was nice.

Then one of the birds dive-bombed them.

Rusty and Mia both covered their faces. The bird flew right past them, then did it again. Rusty wanted to knock it out of the sky, but he didn't want to leave an eye uncovered with which to see the bird, so they settled for keeping their faces covered and hoping that the bird would go away.

The bird landed on Rusty's hand and pecked at his wrist.

He smashed it against the tree.

He dropped the squished bird to the ground. The wolves left it alone.

Rusty wiped the bird's guts off on his jeans. Since much of these pants were burned away, he doubted he would be wearing them again, so some smeared goo didn't really matter.

The other birds stayed away. Rusty hoped that they'd witnessed what happened to their friend and would spread the word that these two treed humans were not to be messed with.

He brushed away more ants.

"They're good protein if we can't get down," Mia noted.

"We can't drink them, though."

"Right, right. Dehydration. Joy."

"The wolves might leave and they might not. Personally, I'm less concerned about dying of thirst than falling asleep—no way will I balance myself well enough not to drop right out of this tree. And if they don't leave until nightfall, we're stuck trying to walk to the truck in the dark, which is why we stayed so long in the cabin in the first place."

"So what's your point?" asked Mia. Rusty didn't take it personally that she sounded pissy.

"My point is that, as far as I'm concerned, we're just resting. After we catch our breath, it's time to start dismembering some wolves."

"How?"

"It's no different than what we did on the front porch, except that it's harder to maneuver and we don't have a cabin burning behind us. As long as we can reach further with the axe than they can reach with their claws, we'll eventually win. And maybe I'll get the chainsaw started again."

"If you get the chainsaw started again, one of us will probably lop off the branch we're sitting on."

"That sounds exactly right. Still, I think we can do it."

"What about jumping from tree to tree?"

"I won't be jumping from tree to tree, sorry. It's just not gonna happen. I won't stop you from trying, but your Uncle Rusty knows his limits."

Mia looked over at the nearest tree. "Yeah, we'd break a few bones trying it. And I'd miss completely. It was a stupid idea."

"The only stupid ideas are the ones you don't share."

"What?"

"No, I was thinking of 'the only stupid questions are the ones you don't ask.' It's something teachers say to make kids feel better about asking stupid questions. There are lots of stupid ideas that you should keep to yourself. Yours wasn't one of them, though—if we can't get rid of the wolves, we may very well have to jump from tree to tree."

"The wolves would just follow us."

"Yes, they would. It'll be a really bad time in our lives."

"How long do you need to rest?" Mia asked.

"If no more birds attack, I'll be good in a couple of minutes."

"Do you want me not to talk during that time?"

"Yeah, let's just sit here. I mean, call out a warning if you need to, obviously."

"Okay."

They sat silently on their branches. Rusty thought he might have heard a slight cracking sound beneath him, but decided that he'd imagined it.

A couple of minutes later, he didn't feel particularly rested, but the aches and pains weren't going to go away before nightfall, so it was time to act. Now the trick was to get the chainsaw out of his backpack without dropping it or falling off the branch.

Mia took out the axe.

Rusty successfully got the chainsaw out of his backpack without a moment of bumbling incompetence. He placed it on his lap, intelligently pointing the blade away from him instead of toward him. He unscrewed the gas cap and peered inside.

"Is it out?" Mia asked.

"No. There's plenty."

"Why won't it start?"

"I don't know. Maybe it's clogged with wolf fur."

The blade *was* looking pretty nasty. Rusty used his index finger to try to get as much gook off of it as he could. As he did so, he had an irrational fear that the chainsaw motor would roar to life, slicing his finger right off, but that wasn't how chainsaws worked and consciously he knew he'd be fine.

"Let's see how this goes," he said, tugging the cord. The chainsaw did not start. He tried again. Still no luck. So it wasn't that anything was clogged, it was that the chainsaw was a piece of crap and he should've bought a new one much sooner, but he was a cheap bastard and didn't like to replace things until they were irreparably broken.

He continued to tug the cord, being as careful as possible not to lose his balance in the process. "Death by deer" would've been a humiliating way to go, but it couldn't compare to "death by slipping while tugging a chainsaw cord." The chainsaw would make the wolf-dismembering process go much more efficiently, and he didn't want to give up until he was positive that the chainsaw was good for nothing but dropping on a wolf's head.

He'd lost track of how many times he pulled the cord when the engine sputtered.

That was good. He could work with a sputter. A sputter meant there was still hope.

He kept tugging. Mia obviously thought it was time to accept the harsh reality of the chainsaw's demise, but she didn't say anything, and Rusty was determined to keep going. He wasn't at the point of whispering sweet nothings to the chainsaw to encourage it to start, but he was getting close.

During this time, they discussed their plan. It was very straightforward: climb down as low as they could get while remaining out of reach of the wolves, then fuck up the wolves as much as possible from there. It would take a while, but as long as they didn't misjudge the distance or tumble from the branch, they should be okay, unless the branch broke or another bird attacked them or zombie squirrels emerged from higher branches or the tree caught fire.

The chainsaw started.

Rusty wondered why neither of them had suggested that they should start the chainsaw *after* climbing down to the proper branch. Then he remembered: they were exhausted and stressed out and not inclined to make wise decisions.

They climbed down a couple of branches. It was tricky with a roaring chainsaw but Rusty made it without a mishap.

Three of the wolves stretched up to their full heights and swiped their claws at them.

A swing of the chainsaw and one of the paws was gone.

The process of awkwardly taking out eight wolves with an axe and a chainsaw while staying out of their reach was not a speedy one. There was a great deal of missing involved. And more than one close call, including one where Rusty would have pitched forward and fallen onto the wolves had Mia not grabbed and steadied him in time.

But they had nowhere else to be. And the pile of moving wolf parts grew larger and larger.

Their greatest asset was the wolves' lack of fear. If the wolves had thought to themselves, *"Shit, this is working out poorly for us, let's move back out of the way of those weapons and wait for our victims to fall out of the tree,"* Rusty and Mia would've been screwed. Instead, they continued to claw at them, even amidst severed paws, limbs, and parts of heads. Eventually only seven wolves were actively mobile, then six, then five, and so on until Rusty finally got the last one in the front left shoulder, slicing off its leg and causing it to topple to the ground, thrashing around but unable to walk.

Rusty and Mia each breathed a sigh of relief. Rusty shut off the chainsaw.

The problem *now* was that the bottom of the tree was piled high with writhing wolf parts. The wolves couldn't come up after them, or follow them along the road, but Rusty wasn't sure how they were going to get down without having to wade through them. There were plenty of snapping jaws and swiping claws down there.

They might have to consider jumping to the next tree.

"No," said Mia.

"What?"

"I see the way you're looking at the other tree."

"We need a way out."

"One of us could break a leg."

"It was your idea in the first place."

"And now I've had time to think about it. If we jump to the next tree, at least one of us will break a leg. Probably you—no offense."

"None taken."

"So we need to figure out something else."

"You mean like jumping down into the wolf parts pile and hoping for the best?"

"I was thinking more about being smart about it and prepared."

Rusty glanced down. Some of the wolves were still thrashing around pretty vigorously. Rusty would feel perfectly safe if he were standing twenty feet away, but jumping down amidst those bodies seemed really freaking dangerous.

But, yeah, he'd break his leg for sure if he tried to leap to the other tree. And then Mia would have to shoot him like a horse.

Instead of leaping to another tree, they could try to jump as far out as possible, hoping to make it past the worst of the wolf remnants. But Rusty could see that turning out very badly. He'd jump, his knee would pop, and he'd fall face-first into the open mouth of a severed wolf head. He'd be chewed up and swallowed without even the consolation prize of knowing that he provided nutrition.

The other option was: climb down. That made them the most vulnerable to the dismembered wolves, but was the least likely to leave them with broken legs, and thus utterly boned.

That was basically it, unless they counted "Hang out in the tree awaiting the merciful release of a slow agonizing death" or "See if a helicopter shows up" as options.

"We just have to climb down there," said Rusty.

"Yeah."

This was going to suck, but they'd done a great many things over the past few hours that sucked, and this was going to suck less than a couple of them. "One at a time, or both at the same time?"

Mia considered that for a moment. "Both at the same time."

"Ready?"

Mia nodded. There were no flecks of blood this time.

Rusty climbed down the tree, taking great care not to step on a wolf torso. One of the wolves immediately spun around on the ground, moving with remarkable haste for an animal missing both of its front legs. Rusty kicked it in the head and hurriedly stepped away.

He narrowly avoided two claw swipes from two different wolves. Mia let out a loud wince. Rusty wasn't sure what had happened to her, but she kept on moving, so it couldn't have been too ghastly.

A wolf that was missing the entire left side of its head tried to bite Rusty's leg. Its jaws did indeed close upon him, but it couldn't get any serious chomping power behind the bite, and Rusty pulled free without a problem.

He slammed his foot down upon the jaws of a severed wolf head, discouraging its biting attempt. Honestly, now that he was down here amongst the wolf parts, it was less dangerous than flat-out *disturbing*. He didn't think he was seconds away from death, but when the inevitable nightmares began, these moments would definitely get more than their share of dream time.

Mia cried out. She raised her foot, which had a wolf head attached to it, then did a high kick, flinging the head away.

"Did it bite you?" Rusty asked.

"Not bad. Don't worry about me."

A severed paw ineffectually tried to murder Rusty, and then he was clear of the wolf parts. A few more steps and Mia was clear as well. They hurried over to the boards they'd dropped, picked them back up, and continued on their way.

"How bad did you get bit?" Rusty asked.

"It didn't break through my shoe. Did you get bit?"

"Only by half a mouth. It didn't do anything."

"We came out of that one okay, then."

"Yeah. And we came out of the porcupine herd okay. We're doing better. Hard to believe it was the—" Rusty started to note the irony that it was a woodpecker that had caused the worst injury, but he didn't think Mia would appreciate that particular observation right now. He'd save that for after the greatest eye surgeon in the world repaired her. "I'm a little haunted by this last one. How about you?"

"Totally haunted," said Mia. "How far do you think we've gone?"

"Not very."

"A mile?"

Rusty didn't think so. "Maybe."

"I have to admit, I feel a little better about this now."

"Why?"

"We have a plan of action. If things get really bad, we can climb a tree and fight them from a safe distance. It wasn't easy or convenient, but we're still alive."

"Some animals can climb trees."

"Right, but some of them *can't*. For the ones that can't, like the packs of wolves that are giving us trouble, we have a plan."

"Fair enough," said Rusty. "Yes, we're better off than we were before we were forced up a tree."

"Bears can climb trees, but it would be climbing the tree vertically, meaning you'd have a chance to slam the chainsaw blade into its head. That's way better than fighting one right in the middle of the road, which we've already done."

"When you put it that way, I guess things are looking up for us."

"We've gone through too much to die now. It wouldn't be fair. We're going to keep on fighting our way through these fuckers, climbing trees when we have to, and then we'll drive the hell out of here. How's your squirrel bite?"

Rusty scratched it. "It's fine. I'd forgotten about it, actually."

"See? You're not going to turn into a zombie."

"Well, we don't know how long it would take, but no, I'm not feeling sick or anything."

"Things are good."

"I wouldn't say good..."

"I got stabbed in the eyeball. It still really, really hurts. If I can say that things are going to work out okay, then you should believe me."

"Then I believe you."

"I tried hopeless bleak despair. I didn't enjoy it. I much prefer the attitude that we're going to kick ass."

"All right," said Rusty. "Then let's kick ass."

CHAPTER EIGHTEEN

They walked for quite a while without anything else attacking them. In fact, Rusty estimated that they were halfway to the truck before a bobcat—the entirety of its spine exposed—ran out of the woods toward them. There wasn't time to start up the chainsaw, but one smack with each of their boards and a few quick swings of Mia's axe took care of it.

The occasional bird swooped down at them. Fortunately, it was never a Hitchcock-style mass of birds; two at the most. They protected their eyes, and though they each got a couple of pecks (and yes, Mia completely freaked out when it happened) they were able to dispatch the birds with relative ease. "Relative" compared to a zombie bear, sure, but the birds fell to the ground with one hit, and from there they could be crushed with a board.

"I used to like birds," said Mia.

"Maybe someday you'll like them again."

"I don't think so."

They heard something running behind them, and when they turned around it was the wolf with the broken neck. Somehow it had followed them all this way, even though its head was flopping back and forth. Rusty wondered how many trees it had bonked into.

Rusty had stopped feeling bad about sawing up the undead forest creatures, but he did kind of feel guilty that the wolf had persevered in the face of adversity and would be rewarded for its fierce tenacity by getting its head chopped off. But unless the wolf turned around and ran in the other direction, it was getting its head chopped off.

The wolf did not turn around.

Rusty pulled the chainsaw cord. It started right up.

The wolf ran toward them, weaving around the road because of the difficulties involved in locating prey when one's head was dangling sideways. It ran past them, realized it overshot its target, did a U-turn, then ran at Rusty.

He sliced its head off.

The remainder of the wolf ran off the road, smacked into a tree, and fell over. Its legs kicked in the air as it struggled to get back up.

Rusty and Mia continued on their way.

Something huge rustled in the bushes to the left.

They glanced over. Another grizzly bear.

Shit.

Rusty revved up the chainsaw. The bear turned and ran, disappearing from sight within seconds.

It must've been a normal bear. A throwback to a simpler time when a bear wouldn't charge at you with homicidal intent unless its cubs were on the other side.

Rusty turned off the chainsaw. "Maybe we're out of the danger zone," he said. "Maybe it's just normal bears from now on."

"I would like that," said Mia.

"Let's see how it goes."

That theory was disproven by the undead raccoon that scampered down a tree and rushed at them. It took an extremely long time to chop the raccoon in half.

Rusty and Mia walked for at least five minutes without anything scary jumping out at them. It was a very pleasant five minutes.

"How far do you think we've gone?" Mia asked.

"I'd say we've passed the two-mile mark. If we keep up this pace, we'll be there in fifteen or twenty minutes."

"What if I ran ahead?"

"Why would you do that?"

"I could get the boards set up. Try to get the truck out. Save us some time."

"No," said Rusty. "I wouldn't want you running up ahead without the chainsaw, and if a zombie bear came after me while you were gone, I wouldn't want you to have the chainsaw."

"I've got the axe."

"The axe is fine, but it's no chainsaw."

"You're right, you're right," said Mia. "Guess I'm just anxious."

"I hear you. But we've made it this far. We'll make it to the end."

"That's what the wolf with the broken neck thought."

Rusty chuckled. "I thought you weren't doing despair anymore."

"I'm not. I agree with you—we'll make it to the end. The way things have been going, we may even make it without having to dismember anything else."

"I've gotta say, as soon as we're out of these woods, I never want to dismember anything again for as long as I live."

"Oh, me too. My dismemberment days are over. I used to love it, but there's only so much dismemberment you can do before you get completely sick of it. Maybe in a few years I'll rediscover my love of dismembering things, but right now I can't imagine ever going at it with the same passion."

"We have weird-ass conversations," Rusty noted.

"I think normal conversations are over for us."

"You're right. How can I ask you to pass the salt after watching you ride around on a zombie bear?"

"I didn't ride around on it," said Mia.

"You were on its back."

"It wasn't a ride."

"When I tell the story, you'll have been riding on the back of a zombie bear."

"I honestly don't feel like this is an adventure that needs to be exaggerated when you tell people about it. If anything, you may want to reign it in."

"Do you know how many body parts we've left behind?" Rusty asked. "Pretty sure people will be able to verify our story."

"You're right."

Rustling in the woods up ahead. Rusty hated that sound. "Shit."

They looked over at the source of the sound. A deer—a buck—emerged from the forest and stood in the middle of the road.

"Normal deer?" Mia asked.

"I'm not sure." They kept walking. The deer didn't move. It stared at them with eyes that may or may not have been bloodshot.

"Get out of here!" Mia shouted. She picked up a rock and flung it at the deer. The rock bounced off its chest. The deer did not run away.

"Undead deer," said Rusty.

He didn't want to be frightened of a deer, but it *did* have antlers that could fuck somebody up.

Rusty hadn't even finished thinking, "*At least it's only one deer*" before a doe stepped into the road next to it. There was no need to question the doe's alive/undead status—ribs were exposed on each side.

Rusty and Mia didn't stop walking. Mia held up her axe and Rusty dropped his board and started the chainsaw, which hadn't given him any more trouble since their escapade in the tree.

Both deer charged.

Rusty didn't panic. A pair of zombie deer were no big deal, not after everything they'd encountered.

They were pretty frickin' fast, though.

The deer seemed to have chosen their individual targets. The buck was coming after Rusty and the doe was coming after Mia. Divided along gender lines. That seemed fair.

Rusty held his ground. He'd use the tactic that had been working reasonably well so far: wait until the last moment, then dodge the charge and swing the chainsaw. As long as he didn't get impaled by those gigantic, razor-sharp-looking antlers (he knew they weren't really razor-sharp, but they sure as hell looked that way when they were headed straight for him at great speed) he'd be fine.

He dodged at the last moment. As the buck raced past him, he swung the chainsaw, opening it up from chest to tail. No guts spilled out, but he'd cut deep, and the buck stumbled as it tried to turn around for a second attack.

Mia was not so fortunate.

Either she hadn't dodged properly or the doe shifted direction, but it had collided with her at full force. She'd fallen to the ground and the doe ran over her, its back legs slamming down on her own legs. Mia screamed.

The doe spun around and trampled her again.

Rusty wanted to pull her to safety, but he still had a vicious buck to contend with. It rushed at him, its mouth wide-open, exposing teeth that shouldn't have been as scary as they were. Rusty stepped out of the way, took a swing at its neck, and missed.

Mia frantically tried to crawl out from underneath the doe. She'd dropped her axe. Rusty couldn't tell how badly she was hurt.

The buck charged again, head lowered, clearly going for impalement. Rusty cried out as one of its antlers struck his shoulder. His whole arm went numb and the chainsaw fell out of his hand, still spinning. He almost lost his footing but stayed upright.

Mia grabbed for the axe. Rusty saw her patting her hand against the ground, unable to see the weapon. The doe leaned down and bit her on the arm. She screamed again.

Rusty couldn't move his fingers. At least his shoulder wasn't bleeding.

The buck came at him once more. The murderous deer wasn't paying enough attention to where it was going, because its front hoof landed on the chainsaw blade. The deer fell over, and Rusty rolled out of the way just in time to avoid being crushed by it.

Rusty snatched up the chainsaw with his non-numb hand and immediately pressed the blade against the buck's neck. After the blade went all the way through, he dropped the chainsaw and picked up the buck's head, which was shockingly heavy.

As the severed head tried to take a big bite out of him, he slammed its antlers into the side of the doe with as much force as he could possibly muster. The antlers, which were not razor-sharp, didn't plunge into the doe, but the impact was enough to distract it from Mia.

It tried to bite Rusty. He thrust the antlers at its head, hoping to gouge out one or both of its eyes. Instead, one of the antlers got the doe right in the snout, sinking deep into its nostril and splitting its snout in half. Rusty let go of the buck's head, which dropped to the ground, still trying to bite. He stomped on its lower jaw, because he was sure that if he didn't he'd accidentally step in its mouth later and lose a toe.

Mia finally got a hold of the axe. She sat up and threw it at the doe. It was a good hit, striking the deer in the side and sinking in deep enough to stick, but throwing the axe wasn't an intelligent decision. She wasn't thinking straight.

The doe slammed its head into Rusty, knocking him to the ground.

It leaned down to bite his face off. He put up his arm in time to block it.

Rusty grabbed the chainsaw and thrust it up into the doe's throat. With no small amount of effort, he sawed off its head, which landed right on his stomach. He turned his head to the side and vomited.

The headless deer walked past him.

He couldn't let it get away with the axe. He got up, fell back down, got up again, and walked after it. The deer was walking faster than he was.

Rusty picked up the buck's head by the antlers and flung it at the doe. The throw didn't have enough distance and the head landed on the ground, breaking one of the antlers.

Rusty doubled over and threw up again. Though this wasn't the worst pain he'd felt today, it was like being punched in the stomach really, really hard. That wasn't something that faded quickly.

The doe wandered off the road. Finally it tripped and fell over.

Rusty walked over to it, wrenched the axe out of its side, chopped off one of its legs to keep it from getting up and following him, then returned to Mia, whose face was contorted in pain. He crouched down next to her, looking for spurting blood.

"Where did it get you?"

"My leg."

Rusty gently ran his hand down her right leg. *Please don't let me feel protruding bones. Please don't let me feel protruding bones. Please don't let me feel protruding bones.*

Her leg seemed okay from this cursory examination. That didn't mean the bones weren't shattered inside.

They needed to get going, but if her leg was in terrible shape, standing her up would make things much worse. He used the axe blade to slice her jeans open to the top of her leg, then pulled the fabric aside.

He stopped the wince in time, though she probably saw him cringe.

There was a hideous bruise that covered her leg from her knee to her waist. He didn't see any spots where the skin was broken, but the whole thing was a truly grotesque mix of red and dark purple. It wasn't difficult to imagine thousands of bone splinters underneath that mess.

"Do you think it's broken?" Rusty asked.

"I don't know."

"I'm going to very slowly help you up. If you feel like it's grinding things around in there, we'll stop and figure out something else. Okay?"

"Okay."

Rusty took both of her hands and stood up. He gradually began to pull her up, expecting a shriek of agony at any moment. She whimpered in pain, but did not wail as if broken bones were stabbing into muscles.

Finally she was on her feet. With Rusty still holding her, she took a tentative step forward.

"I—I don't think I broke anything."

"Thank God."

"I don't know if I can walk on it, though."

"Let's test it out."

Rusty didn't let go of her hands, but he relaxed his grip so that she was mostly staying upright on her own. She started to take a step, then shook her head. "I can't walk. I can't put my full weight on that leg or I'm gonna lose my balance."

"Okay...well...that's unfortunate, but we'll work through it. I can carry you on my back."

"You can *not* carry me on your back."

"Not easily."

"You can barely walk yourself. We have to find another way."

"We can hide you and I can come back for you after I get the truck."

"We already decided that splitting up was bad."

"Right," said Rusty. "It is bad. But if you can't walk..."

"I'll use one of the boards as a crutch. If that doesn't work, you can bury me in the mud or something until you get back."

"Is the board the right height?"

"We'll see."

The board was a little too short to make a good crutch, but it made a usable-if-awkward one, and at least Mia could walk. She put the axe in her backpack. Rusty didn't like her not having it immediately handy, but he expected Mia to fall at least once and probably several times and he didn't want it to happen while she was holding a sharp bladed weapon. He picked up the board he'd dropped. He'd known they were good for being made into furniture, but boards were proving to be useful in so very many ways.

"It's nothing to worry about," Rusty assured her.

"We're less than a mile away. We'll make it. It'll just take longer, that's all. No big deal."

The board slipped out from under Mia and she fell to the ground. Rusty helped her up and they continued walking.

"I don't know if my eye or my leg is worse," said Mia.

"Your eye."

"I'm going to need surgery on both. Who do you think will have a longer hospital stay? You'll have skin grafts."

"I don't want to talk about hospitals," said Rusty.

"All right. What do you want to talk about?"

"Nothing, if at all possible."

"It's not. If I don't talk, I'm going to stay inside my own head, and it's not a pretty place right now."

"Let's talk about food."

"Okay."

Progress was shitty.

Mia fell three more times, once really badly, but each time she got right up and forced herself to continue onward. Rusty wasn't entirely convinced that she hadn't broken anything, and that each step was ruining her leg even more, but she insisted that she wanted to go on. He really didn't want to leave her behind. If he got the truck, came back, and found her half-devoured by the wildlife, he wasn't sure that he wouldn't just rev up the chainsaw and slam his face into the blade.

Still, it was starting to feel like they might never reach the truck.

They hadn't discussed what they'd do if they couldn't

get the truck out of the mud. Walking the rest of the way to town wasn't within any realm of possibility. They'd simply have to wait inside the vehicle for help that would almost certainly never arrive. A slow, horrible death, unless they made a pact to hasten the process.

That was two suicide scenarios in a row. Rusty needed to think about something else, though talking about delicious food with Mia was honestly making him kind of miserable.

The bobcat that went after him was in worse shape than any of the animals they'd encountered thus far, so rotted away that in one spot Rusty could actually see a pinpoint of sunlight shining through its side.

It pounced at him, knocking him to the ground.

It tore its claws across his chest, pulling several of the strips of wood loose. They'd held on admirably well, but the combination of perspiration and animals clawing at them was finally too much.

The bobcat's severed head dropped onto him. Pain exploded in Rusty's face as its front teeth smashed into his nose. He batted the head away before it could start chewing on him. Mia fell next to him.

Rusty ran his hand across his nose and looked at his bloody palm. "Goddamn it," he said, slightly muffled.

"I'm sorry."

"Not your fault. I should've chainsawed it before it knocked me down." The rest of the bobcat had flopped over on its side, but its claws were still dangerous, so Rusty started up the chainsaw and removed them. He shut off the chainsaw as Mia returned the axe to her backpack and replaced the board crutch.

"Your nose is bleeding bad," she said.

Rusty wiped some blood away. "Yeah, that's what

happens when a bobcat head falls on it."

The next half hour was far from effortless, but they did not break any bones, lose any limbs, or bleed to death. That was Rusty's bar for success now. If they weren't dragging themselves along the dirt road by their teeth, they were doing okay.

They were approaching a very familiar curve. Unless Rusty was mistaken, which was entirely possible, when they rounded this curve they'd be in sight of the truck.

They rounded the curve. The truck was just where they'd left it.

"Are those—?" Mia started to ask.

"No," said Rusty, even though, yeah, it looked like the mud around the truck was swarming with snakes.

CHAPTER NINETEEN

In the grand scheme of things, there were far worse things that could be "guarding" the truck than snakes, even zombie snakes. Rusty wasn't inclined to run down a mental list at the moment, but without a doubt, snakes were a minor concern. Neither he nor Mia had an irrational paralyzing fear of the reptiles, they wouldn't withstand a good whacking with the boards, and they'd simply make it a point to be extremely careful and not get bit. It wasn't as good as there being *nothing* dangerous around the truck, but ultimately it wasn't all that bad.

As they walked forward, Rusty heard rustling in the back of the truck.

Lots of rustling.

He suspected that this wasn't good rustling.

"Hold on," he told Mia. "I don't think it's just the snakes."

They stood there, listening closely.

"Did you hear a snort?" asked Mia.

"No."

"I thought I heard a snort."

"I hear something moving in the back of the truck."

A squirrel peeked its head over the edge of the cargo bed.

And then another.

And another.

"No," said Mia. "No, this is not okay with me."

The first squirrel jumped out of the truck and scurried toward Rusty and Mia, followed by the second. And then there was a whole flood of squirrels pouring out of the back of the truck—dozens of bloodshot eyes headed toward them.

Mia readied her board while Rusty started the chainsaw.

There were so many of them. This was insane. Had they just been sleeping in the back of the truck this whole time, hoping somebody would stop by? Did they smell the scent of the first squirrel and hope to avenge his gruesome death?

The squirrels reached them.

Mia swung the board, bashing the closest squirrel's brains out but not stopping it from scampering back at her. She immediately lost her balance, but used the board to brace herself just in time. If she fell, she'd be engulfed by squirrels. They'd skeletonize her like piranha skeletonizing a cow.

Rusty waved the chainsaw around his legs, sending squirrel limbs flying into the air. At first he was doing a fine job of keeping them away, but there were too many of them. One scampered up his left leg while another scampered up his right. He successfully grabbed one of them by the tail and tossed it onto the chainsaw blade, cutting the squirrel in half, but the other one ran up his back and into his hair.

He jabbed the chainsaw blade at it, making sure not to press the blade into his scalp. Part of a squirrel slid down the side of his face.

Mia crushed three squirrels in rapid succession. *Splat! Splat! Splat!* That left plenty more.

Two more squirrels ran up Rusty's leg. Then three. Then one was gnawing on his ear in the least sensual manner imaginable.

Rusty waved the chainsaw around like a slasher movie psychopath, lopping off at least two squirrel pieces with each swing. They just kept coming, as if the back of the truck was a portal to another dimension in which an infinite number of squirrels resided. (Rusty was sure this wasn't really the case—he was just a bit overwhelmed at the moment.)

He added violent stomping to the mix, crushing one's skull and breaking another's back.

Squirrels were no longer pouring out of the back of the truck, so it wasn't a dimensional portal. There were still a fuckload of them.

Rusty continued to swing the chainsaw blade at squirrels that were currently crawling on him. It was insanely risky, but he didn't really have another choice. He had thus far managed to avoid slicing off one of his own body parts, and he wasn't inclined to put down the chainsaw right now. It had served him well thus far.

Mia got in a really good hit that sent a porcupine quill all the way through a squirrel's head. They'd have to pluck the quills out before they used the boards to get the truck out of the mud, so this saved some time.

Rusty cut off a squirrel's tail, which wasn't his intent. The tail spun around on the ground like a battery powered cat toy.

Mia bashed a squirrel to mush. Another squirrel crawled onto the splatter, and became mush along with it.

In a single wide sweep of the chainsaw, Rusty bisected five different squirrels. Mia's head was turned when he did this, so she missed this astounding accomplishment. It didn't really matter, and of course he had far more important things to worry about than whether or not his niece witnessed the quintuple dismemberment, but it was still a bit frustrating.

Mia lost her balance again. This time the board didn't stop her fall.

She landed face-first. At least ten squirrels pounced upon her at once, their tiny claws and teeth ripping at the back of her shirt.

Rusty went into action with the chainsaw. He couldn't *tell* her not to move over the sound of the motor, but he was pretty sure she'd get the message. He waved the chainsaw to and fro, slicing squirrels while being incredibly careful not to cut his niece. The pieces, of course, continued to move, but most of them would fall off when she stood back up. A couple of the squirrels were kind enough to run into the blade on their own, while others required more effort. During this process, Rusty had squirrels crawling on him as well, but Mia was his top priority right now.

Finally he'd gotten them all except for one asshole squirrel that was particularly agile. Mia could handle that one. He moved away and she stood up, frantically brushing moving squirrel parts off of her.

Rusty resumed work on his own problems. Mutilating squirrels on his own body with a chainsaw was much trickier than mutilating squirrels on somebody else's body with a chainsaw, and one of them had wrapped itself in his thinning hair so tightly that it stayed in place even when the top half of its body fell away.

They were biting the hell out of him. The squirrel bite from before had been a nagging source of stress in the back of his mind since it happened, but now he had several dozen bites to go along with it. He wouldn't worry about that right now. He couldn't. He needed to stay sane until they got to town.

A squirrel managed a particularly deep bite on his leg, pressing its mouth against his skin as if it was trying to burrow its entire head in there. He jabbed the chainsaw blade at it. The squirrel leapt off his leg, and the chainsaw blade grazed his thigh.

It wasn't as if a huge spray of blood jettisoned from the limb, but there was blood.

He managed to keep his hold on the chainsaw, grit his teeth, and resume the process of squirrel destruction. If anything, he was even angrier at them now.

Mia smashed the corner of the board into that wretched squirrel. Both of its bloodshot eyes popped out of their sockets. She smashed it several more times— there was clearly an element of vengeance involved. By the time she was done, the squirrel would never again leap from somebody's leg at an inopportune time.

They were running out of squirrels to massacre.

None of them fled, so Rusty and Mia didn't have to chase any of them down. They just stood where they were and the squirrels came to them. And a few minutes later, the ground was littered with writhing squirrel parts, along with various moist but not bleeding splotches that used to be functioning rodents.

Rusty shut off the chainsaw. There was a *lot* of goo on

the blade.

"How's your leg?" Mia asked.

"It's fine," Rusty said, as several trickles of blood ran down from the wound.

"Can you walk?"

"I can walk to the truck. That's all we need to do."

Something snorted.

"Did you hear it that time?" Mia asked.

"Yeah. Zombie wild hog? I think we should get the truck out of the mud and get out of here."

"I agree with that plan."

Something moved behind the truck.

"If I can get rid of eight million squirrels, I can handle a pig," said Rusty, pulling the chainsaw cord. It roared to life, sputtered, and died. He pulled the cord a couple more times and nothing happened. He unscrewed the gas cap and looked inside.

"Is it empty?" Mia asked.

"Yeah. That's pretty disappointing." He set the chainsaw on the ground.

"Do you want the axe?"

"That's probably a good idea."

Mia took the axe out of her backpack and handed it over.

Another snort.

"Here, piggy, piggy, piggy," Rusty called out. "Come on out or I'll huff and I'll puff and I'll blow your house in."

"You really got yourself good," said Mia, pointing to Rusty's bleeding leg.

"I know. It's okay. I'll still be able to drive, no problem. The more I bleed now, the less blood I'll get all over the truck."

The hog emerged from behind the truck.

That is, the *hogs* emerged.

That is, the...what the fuck *was* that?

From a purely technical sense, you could say that three wild hogs and two red foxes walked out from behind the truck. But they were fused together, covered with an unidentified clear viscous liquid. So instead of five separate animals, it was one nightmare animal with five heads and twenty legs. Had they all died at the same time and gotten stuck when they returned? Were they...actually, Rusty had no other theories for the origin of this creature that stood before them. It was there and Rusty was about to shit his pants and nothing else was important.

"Are you seeing what I'm seeing?" asked Mia.

"Yes."

"Because I've only got one working eye, so I may just be seeing it wrong."

"Nope, you're seeing a giant pig/fox monster."

"Maybe it's blood loss. We're both bleeding pretty bad. Eventually we'd start to have visions, right?"

"I don't think we'd be having visions of the same monster. We live together and we've shared a lot of the same experiences, but I don't see us both having visions of a three-pig two-fox mutant zombie."

"You're probably right."

"Yeah, I am. It's real."

"Shit."

The abomination against God began to move toward them. Since it was trying to coordinate five sets of legs, its movements were somewhat awkward, though not bumbling enough to provide any measure of comic relief.

All three of the hog heads began to snort. Rusty did

not speak pig but these were clearly hostile snorts. The red foxes made no noise, but they opened and closed their mouths, apparently to show off their impressively sharp teeth.

Rusty and Mia each took a step back.

"It's kind of slow," said Rusty. "Maybe we can lead it away from the truck instead of fighting it."

They kept backing up. The monstrosity followed.

It was picking up speed, as if the five bodies were quickly learning how to work together. Since neither Rusty nor Mia were in any condition to run away, the "lead it away from the truck" plan quickly disappeared as a viable strategy.

Could it even hurt them? Regular zombie red foxes could pounce on you and slash at you with their paws and bite your throat out. Rusty wasn't sure this thing could even bend any of its heads down that far. Perhaps its greatest danger came from the possibility that you'd just stand there, paralyzed, going "*What the fuck is that?*"

"The boards aren't gonna do it," Mia said, right before her bad leg twisted beneath her and she fell over.

Rusty thought of another potential origin story for the creature. A farmer with too much time on his hands captured three pigs and two foxes and glued them together. This was not a credible origin, but Rusty liked it better than the thought that the ground had split open, spewing lava, and a demon crawled out from the pits of hell.

Rusty reached down, intending to help Mia up, but there was no time. He was going to have to take the offensive on his own.

He raised the axe and walked forward.

Hogs had always creeped him out, just a little. Even if

he ignored the fact that they were part of a five-headed demon, they were way creepier than normal hog heads because of the bloodshot eyes.

He had nothing clever to say, and didn't care. He wasn't sure if he should start chopping at the middle head, or pick one on the end and work his way down the line. He decided to start with the hog on the left.

He swung the axe at its neck. It was enough to make a huge dent, but not enough to sever the head. Blackish yellow goo sprayed from the wound—apparently the mutant version of the zombie animals had extra liquid inside. The hog let out an ear-piercing squeal.

Rusty yanked the axe out of its neck and slammed it down again. It was an equally strong hit, but he was off by a few inches, so the hog's head remained attached. It's squealing got even louder, making Rusty cringe.

The parts of the animal on the right side began to move, while the hog on the left remained standing where it was. Rusty struck it with the axe a third time. This hit landed in the gap created by the first blow, but it still wasn't enough to decapitate the hog. The other two hog heads also began to squeal, a sound that was worse than scraping fingernails along a chalkboard until the nails snapped off and the jagged edges continued to scrape along the chalkboard for eternity.

By the time Rusty realized what the rest of the creature was doing, it was too late for him to move his slow injured ass out of the way.

It was surrounding him.

He was now in the middle of a circle-shaped five-headed beast. Not a great place to be. He wished he'd massacred fewer squirrels and saved some chainsaw fuel for this thing.

The hog heads kept squealing.

He chopped the head on what used to be the left once more. Another solid hit, and another hit that didn't quite do the trick. The head was now dangling by strands of pork, but it hadn't yet fallen off.

Rusty raised the axe over his head, preparing to deliver a mighty blow that would downgrade this five-headed monster to a four-headed monster.

The blade of the axe popped off, flying into the air behind him and landing outside the circle of the beast.

Son of a bitch.

They'd asked a lot of the axe today, but couldn't it have lasted for just four more heads?

Rusty decided not to lose his shit quite yet. He grabbed the mostly severed hog head by the ears and ripped it off its neck. Like the deer head, it was heavier than expected, and it fell out of his hands. A massive gout of the blackish yellow goo sprayed from the stump, drenching Rusty. It reeked of pure rot. The head kept moving but at least it wasn't squealing any more, though the other two hogs were contributing plenty to the noise level.

He still had the wooden axe handle. Given a few uninterrupted hours to work, he could probably splatter the remaining heads.

"What can I do?" asked Mia, sounding frantic.

Rusty spat out some goo. "Get the boards in place!"

"Okay!"

"Take the quills out first!"

"I know!"

"Don't get bit by any snakes!"

"I won't!"

Rusty wasn't sure if he should start whacking the

creature with the axe handle or not. The heads weren't actually attacking him right now, and he didn't want to anger them. But he'd just chopped one of them off, so a beating didn't seem like it would make things worse.

The creature began to move forward, meaning some of them moved forward and some of them moved backward, but it came closer to Rusty, who walked in pace with it to keep himself from getting bitten.

He glanced down. Wow, his leg really *was* bleeding badly. Like, "creating a countdown to his death" badly. Once he got out of the nightmare circle, he'd have to not worry about the germs and wrap something around it to slow the bleeding. At least he wasn't...actually, he was feeling a little dizzy, now that he thought about it.

The creature—one hog head and one fox head, specifically—kept moving toward him. Rusty stumbled as he tried to remain in the center of the circle.

If he were in this position twenty-four hours ago, he might've been able to leapfrog over one of the fused animals. Now? No way in hell. He'd be lucky if he could...

Crawling under them might not be a bad idea.

Yeah, he'd get trampled. But it wouldn't be the combined weight of all five bodies. It wouldn't be any worse than being trampled by one of them. The hog would be heavier, but the fox would have sharper claws.

Mia, who thankfully didn't have any snakes dangling from her arms by their fangs, had wedged both planks underneath the back tires of the truck. Now they could gain traction. Now they could drive out of the mud, then enjoy a leisurely road trip out of this forest, waving at undead animals through the window as they passed.

Rusty had to accept that there really was no way out of

this predicament except under their legs.

And once he accepted this, there was no reason to wait.

He dropped to his knees, splitting open his leg wound even worse, and then hurriedly crawled toward a set of legs. He'd chosen one of the foxes.

Maybe he could squeeze past them without getting trampled.

He couldn't. Rusty was moving like a fifty-year-old man with burnt-up legs and a chainsaw gash, and the creature changed direction, so one of the cloven hooves of the hog came down on his left hand. He hadn't necessarily broken *all* of the bones in that hand, but he'd broken many of them.

He continued to crawl forward, a process made more difficult now that he had a broken hand. The hog's foot landed on the same hand in almost the same place. Rusty didn't even shriek, he just silently opened his mouth as wide as it would go.

Through the legs, he could see Mia crouched down on the other side. "Give me your hands!" she said.

Rusty didn't want to give her his hands, but he didn't want to get stomped to death, so he reached for her. She reached for him and grabbed him by the wrists. With her pulling on him and Rusty crawling, he was able to scoot out from underneath the creature and only get stepped on a few dozen times.

He kept crawling even after he was clear of the monster.

Mia tried to pull him to his feet, but he waved her off. "Fuck it," he said. "I'll crawl." Though he didn't think he'd broken anything except his hand, he suspected that the non-bruised parts of his body were now a minority.

Everything hurt. Okay, his tongue didn't hurt. Every part of his body except his goddamn tongue hurt.

The truck wasn't that far. He could make it.

He crawled and crawled, but the creature followed, moving at the same pace.

CHAPTER TWENTY

Rusty had forgotten about the snakes.
He was not fearful of them under normal circumstances, but normal circumstances did not include crawling along the ground where they were lurking. True, he was more concerned about the mutant beast that was pursuing him, but the idea of crawling over snakes to get to the truck held little appeal.

One particularly large one was slithering toward him now.

What kind of venom would an undead snake have? Would it be better or worse than getting bitten by a live one? Rusty hoped to remain blissfully ignorant on this issue.

Mia kicked the snake out of the way.

Another one was right behind it.

Rusty didn't need to look back to see how close the hellspawn was to catching up to him. He could tell that it was right freaking there, and that if he slowed down to avoid an encounter with a snake, he was screwed.

One of its paws or hooves—he didn't look back to see

which—landed on his foot. Rusty pulled free and kept moving forward. The truck was close. So close. So very close that it would be impossibly cruel for him not to make it.

Mia kicked another snake out of the way and stomped on a third. Plenty of snakes remained, and they were clearly undead ones. Normal snakes would not all be slithering straight at Rusty as if hoping to feast upon him.

A snake slithered over his broken hand. He used his good hand to brush it away. It came right back. He grabbed the end of its tail and flung it out of the way.

The hog heads had not quit squealing.

Rusty reached the mud that had been the source of so many of their recent problems. Without this mud, they would have been able to say, "Goodness, the animals in this forest are behaving in a rather quaint manner. Let us proceed to our motor vehicle so that we might drive to a safer location." Fuck mud.

The mud was more like soft deep dirt now, but it was going to make it more difficult to crawl away from the monster that was still right behind him.

Mia opened the truck door. Rusty realized that he was whimpering as he was crawling, which was kind of embarrassing but he assumed he'd get over it. The monster stepped on his foot with a hoof—definitely a hoof this time—and it sunk into the dirt a bit.

He pulled it free. Adrenaline. Oh, how he loved adrenaline. A nice little burst of adrenaline would make everything all better.

Instead, he had Mia.

She grabbed his arms and yanked him to his feet. An intense bolt of pain tore through his body, and he knew she messed up some stuff inside of him, but the alternative was to leave him to get devoured by snakes in the mud, so she'd made the right call.

Mia pushed him toward the open door. Rusty did his part by scrambling into the vehicle.

Mia lost her balance.

Rusty grabbed her before she fell.

One of the fox heads chomped down on her arm.

Then a hog head did the same. A gout of blood sprayed over its porcine face.

The burst of adrenaline kicked in. Rusty pulled Mia into the truck. With him already in the driver's seat and the steering wheel in the way, there wasn't much room to maneuver, but she managed to get on top of him, accidentally honking the horn.

Rusty tried to slam the door shut. It slammed on one of the hog heads, making it squeal even louder. He pushed on its forehead, trying to shove it out of the way, but though it was just one head it had the body strength of five animals, and it wasn't going anywhere.

Mia climbed into the passenger seat.

Rusty punched the hog in the snout.

"Give me a gun!" he said.

Mia opened her backpack and rummaged through it.

Rusty slammed the door twice more on the hog's head, hoping it would take the hint. It didn't. It lunged even further into the truck, trying to take a bite out of Rusty's side.

Mia handed Rusty a pistol.

He pressed it between the hog's eyes and pulled the trigger.

Bone, flesh, and rancid goo exploded from the back of the hog's head. It pulled back.

Rusty slammed the door shut.

The hog bashed its face against the door. Rusty didn't mind a few dents in the truck.

He realized that nothing hurt anymore. Either he was so excited that they might be safe that his brain had called a temporary halt on pain sensors, or he was dead and it didn't matter.

He patted his pocket. No keys.

There were a million opportunities for him to have lost them.

No need to panic. He kept a spare in the glove compartment.

He reached over and popped open the glove compartment. Lots of papers and other assorted items spilled out onto the floor. Mia immediately bent down to start sifting through them to find the key.

The monster kept bashing against the door.

"Here it is," said Mia, handing Rusty the key.

He slid it into the ignition. As he turned the key, he was ninety percent sure the truck wouldn't start, because that was the way things had been going in his life recently, but the engine started right up.

Now he had to get out of the mud. This would be much easier if Mia were standing outside to guide him to make sure that the truck stayed directly on the wooden boards when it backed up, but somehow he didn't think it would be very respectful to ask that of her at the present time.

"Keep your fingers crossed," he said. They weren't completely, irreversibly, unspeakably screwed if the truck remained stuck, but they were pretty damned screwed nevertheless.

He put the truck into reverse.

Rusty placed his hands on the steering wheel. Placing

his broken, now-swollen hand on the wheel brought back all of the pain that had disappeared. So he wasn't dead. Good.

He very gently pressed down on the gas pedal.

The truck didn't move.

He pressed a little more.

Still nothing.

The monster continued to bash its head against the truck door.

Rusty gave it a little more gas.

The truck began to move backwards.

Traction! It had traction! Sweet, glorious, beloved traction!

He needed to stay calm. He didn't want to mess this up by being over confident or in too much of a hurry to drive away from this nightmarish demonic blasphemous monstrosity. Just keep backing up slowly until they were completely out of the mud. No rush.

He kept backing up until he could see the boards in front of the truck.

The monster walked after the vehicle with its twenty legs.

Rusty put the truck into drive.

He wanted nothing more than to floor the gas pedal, smashing the truck directly into the monster at high speed and sending pig and fox parts flying everywhere in a beautiful display of blackish yellow slime. But that would be unwise. The monster would get stuck beneath the undercarriage and he and Mia would be trapped.

Instead, Rusty swerved around it, and then drove off at a reasonable speed.

"I think we made it," said Mia.

"We might have," said Rusty. They still had eleven and a half miles of dirt road to go, which was plenty of time to find a giant zombie grizzly bear blocking the path, but he couldn't deny that he was feeling pretty good right now.

"What do you think we'll find?"

"Doctors, hopefully."

"I mean...do you think this is...you know, a really big problem?"

Rusty sighed. "I would like to believe that there are two victims in this mess: you and me. Everybody else in the world is just going about their regular day."

"But is that what you *do* believe?"

"It doesn't matter what I believe. Either we're going to drive into a zombie-laden hellscape or we're not. We'll deal with it when we get there."

"All right." Mia reached for the visor.

"Don't," Rusty told her.

"What?"

"Don't lower the visor."

"I want to see my—"

"I know what you want to see. Don't look in the mirror." He tilted the rear-view mirror away from her.

"I can always look in the side-view mirror."

"Seriously, wait until you get your face cleaned up. You don't want to see it now. It looks worse than it is."

"Okay." She picked up a napkin off the floor and wiped her face. "Should I go with a patch or a glass eye?"

"A patch would look pretty badass."

"I agree. How's your hand?"

"It's like every single nerve is screaming in pain."

"How are your legs?" Mia asked.

"They hurt, too," said Rusty. "How's your leg?"

"Excruciating. How are all of your bites and scratches?"

"Not as bad as my hand. How are all of *your* bites and scratches?"

"Not as bad as my eye."

Rusty chuckled.

"I think the world is going to be fine," said Mia.

A squirrel ran out in front of the truck. Rusty flattened it and continued driving.

He became more and more optimistic as he drove. No zombie animals had created a barricade in the road. Maybe the world had indeed transformed into an apocalyptic nightmare, but at least they'd get to find out instead of dying in the forest.

They reached the end of the dirt road.

Rusty turned onto the paved road, and they were immediately struck by another truck speeding in the opposite direction.

"Crazy stuff," said the old man. "Crazy, crazy stuff."

Their truck was totaled. The old man's truck was damaged but still drivable, so they were riding with him. Rusty and Mia had both been injured in the accident, but what were a few more bruises, a few more lacerations, and another broken bone in the grand scheme of things?

"They tracked it to this long stream," the old man explained. "The animals drink from the stream. They die, kind of. Their blood dries up and they rot. They go full-on predator and suddenly you can't kill them unless you run 'em over with a steamroller. Crazy stuff. Can't believe how fast it happened. Somebody said they saw two deer stuck together like Siamese twins, if you can believe it."

"How are they going to stop it?" Mia asked.

"If it was up to me, they'd drop a nuke on the area. But it's not up to me. Which I guess is good, because then you've got radiation poisoning and people start oozing and stuff. Instead, they're going to burn it. Burn that forest to the ground. Wipe out everything in it."

Rusty nodded. That sounded reasonable.

Rusty sat on the examination table in his boxer shorts.

"I guess I don't have to ask if you were bit," said the doctor.

"Nope."

"That's going to mean close observation like the others who were bit, but I'm sure you knew you weren't going to be released today anyway."

"Is there any evidence of...?"

"People turning into zombies?"

"Yeah."

"Nah. Better safe than sorry, of course, but so far there's really no indication that these are worse than any other wild animal bites. Wild animal bites can carry their own set of diseases, of course, but we don't believe you will rise from the dead to feast upon the flesh of the living."

"Well, that's a relief," said Rusty.

"Indeed. But we'll have a more concrete update for you in seventy-two hours."

Seventy-three hours later, Mia sat next to Rusty's hospital bed. The doctors had not been able to save her eye. Right now the socket was covered in gauze, with a badass eye patch to follow, and she was in good spirits.

"So I've been thinking about how I was going to send you off to experience life," said Rusty. "My thought is, now that our cabin is gone, along with all of the forest surrounding it, I might come with you."

"I'd like that."

"I mean, I still have to be released from here, which isn't going to happen anytime soon, and we'll get more out of the experience if we wait until we can walk again, but at some point we'll go to a big city and do big-city stuff."

"It's a deal."

"I'm not saying I'm going to become a city dweller. As soon as I can, I'm finding a new forest and building a new cabin. It's going to have a chainsaw in every room."

Mia smiled and gave Rusty a kiss on the cheek. "I'll be proud to live there."

— The End —

ACKNOWLEDGEMENTS

Thanks to Tod Clark, Donna Fitzpatrick, Lynne Hansen, Michael McBride, Jim Morey, Rhonda Rettig, and Paul Synuria II for their zombie-riffic assistance with this novel. They did not read these acknowledgments, which is why "zombie-riffic" was not cut.

Remember:
Readers who leave reviews deserve great big hugs!

Subscribe to Jeff Strand's free monthly newsletter (which includes a brand-new original short story in every issue) at http://eepurl.com/bpv5br

OTHER BOOKS BY JEFF STRAND

Bring Her Back. A tale of revenge and madness.

Sick House. A home invasion from beyond the grave.

Bang Up. A filthy comedic thriller. "You want to pay me to sleep with your wife?" is just the start of the story.

Cold Dead Hands. Ten people are trapped in a freezer during a terrorist attack on a grocery store.

How You Ruined My Life (Young Adult). Sixteen-year-old Rod has a pretty cool life until his cousin Blake moves in and slowly destroys everything he holds dear.

Everything Has Teeth. A third collection of short tales of horror and macabre comedy.

An Apocalypse of Our Own. Can the Friend Zone survive the end of the world?

Stranger Things Have Happened (Young Adult). Teenager Marcus Millian III is determined to be one of the greatest magicians who ever lived. Can he make a live shark disappear from a tank?

Cyclops Road. When newly widowed Evan Portin gives a woman named Harriett a ride out of town, she says she's on a cross-country journey to slay a Cyclops. Is she crazy, or...?

Blister. While on vacation, cartoonist Jason Tray meets the town legend, a hideously disfigured woman who lives in a shed.

The Greatest Zombie Movie Ever (Young Adult). Three best friends with more passion than talent try to make the ultimate zombie epic.

Kumquat. A road trip comedy about TV, hot dogs, death, and obscure fruit.

I Have a Bad Feeling About This (Young Adult). Geeky, non-athletic Henry Lambert is sent to survival camp, which is bad enough *before* the trio of murderous thugs show up.

Pressure. What if your best friend was a killer...and he wanted you to be just like him? Bram Stoker Award nominee for Best Novel.

Dweller. The lifetime story of a boy and his monster. Bram Stoker Award nominee for Best Novel.

A Bad Day For Voodoo. A young adult horror/comedy about why sticking pins in a voodoo doll of your history teacher isn't always the best idea. Bram Stoker Award nominee for Best Young Adult Novel.

Dead Clown Barbecue. A collection of demented stories about severed noses, ventriloquist dummies, giant-sized vampires, sibling stabbings, and lots of other messed-up stuff.

Dead Clown Barbecue Expansion Pack. A few more stories for those who couldn't get enough.

Wolf Hunt. Two thugs for hire. One beautiful woman. And one vicious frickin' werewolf.

Wolf Hunt 2. New wolf. Same George and Lou.

The Sinister Mr. Corpse. The feel-good zombie novel of the year.

Benjamin's Parasite. A rather disgusting action/horror/comedy about why getting infected with a ghastly parasite is unpleasant.

Fangboy. A dark and demented fairy tale for adults.

Kutter. A serial killer finds a Boston terrier, and it might just make him into a better person.

Faint of Heart. To get her kidnapped husband back, Melody has to relive her husband's nightmarish weekend, step-by-step...and survive.

Mandibles. Giant killer ants wreaking havoc in the big city!

Stalking You Now. A twisty-turny thriller soon to be the feature film *Mindy Has To Die.*

Graverobbers Wanted (No Experience Necessary). First in the Andrew Mayhem series.

Single White Psychopath Seeks Same. Second in the Andrew Mayhem series.

Casket For Sale (Only Used Once). Third in the Andrew Mayhem series.

Lost Homicidal Maniac (Answers to "Shirley"). Fourth in the Andrew Mayhem series.

The Andrew Mayhem Collection. All four novels for one low price!

Suckers (with JA Konrath). Andrew Mayhem meets Harry McGlade. Which one will prove to be more incompetent?

Gleefully Macabre Tales. A collection of thirty-two demented tales. Bram Stoker Award nominee for Best Collection.

Elrod McBugle on the Loose. A comedy for kids (and adults who were warped as kids).

The Haunted Forest Tour (with James A. Moore). The greatest theme park attraction in the world! Take a completely safe ride through an actual haunted forest!

Just hope that your tram doesn't break down, because this forest is PACKED with monsters...

Draculas (with JA Konrath, Blake Crouch, and F. Paul Wilson). An outbreak of feral vampires in a secluded hospital. This one isn't much like *Twilight*.

For information on all of these books, visit Jeff Strand's more-or-less official website at JeffStrand.com.

Made in the USA
Middletown, DE
03 September 2019